The Hidden Lives of Dick & Mary

Two Novellas of Supernatural Suspense

XAVIER POE KANE

C2 VISIONARY PRESS

Kane, Xavier Poe, 1975-
The Hidden Lives of Dick & Mary: Two Novellas of Supernatural Suspense / Xavier Poe Kane.
1. Paranormal – Fiction. 2. Missouri – Fiction 3. Domestic – Fiction.

ISBN: 978-1-08794514-9

Library of Congress Cataloging-in-Publication has been applied for.

Any references to historical events, real people, or real places are used fictitiously. All other names, characters, and places are products of the author's imagination.

Edited by Kayla Randolph
Cover Design by Richard Turylo
Interior Layout by Haley Chung

C2 Visionary Press, LLC
St. Louis, Missouri

For Mom, while not the type of book you would've ever read, I could not have written it without your love and support.

Haunted Houses
Gateway to the West and the Beyond

Prologue

Shadows began to darken the office of Lieutenant Colonel Mickey "Logan" Delaney. He checked his phone: 6:25 p.m. The Missouri Air National Guard officer had put in a long day. He took a minute to finish the last email before standing and stretching his six-foot-two-inch frame, which he frequently insisted was not built to be hunched behind a desk. He unzipped his flight suit and changed into jeans and his leather riding jacket.

Winter was surrendering to spring, and the weather had been beautiful. Today's high had reached 72°, so he rode his Harley into work. However, the temperature would not cooperate for long after sunset. He grabbed his helmet and stepped out of his office.

Standard operating procedure was for the last one in the building to secure the exterior doors and ensure all the lights are turned off. As he had countless times before, he started with the second-story fire escape. From there, he checked the three doors on the first floor. He pulled out his phone and used its flashlight to navigate to the basement. He could pop out the single subterranean fire escape to complete the security check. As he started down the stairs, he heard a door slam.

"Hey, sorry. I thought I was the only one left." His voice carried in the empty hall as he paused to greet the other airman working late. "Hello?" He shrugged as his second greeting proved fruitless.

He once again started down the short flight of antique stairs. As he stepped onto the basement floor, a stair creaked behind him. He turned to see who was sneaking up on him, but the bright beam from his cell played over an empty staircase. The air took a sudden chill, causing him to shiver.

"I'm imagining things," he said out loud, trying to convince himself.

He turned on his heel and started down the hallway that ran the length of the building. He could see the soft, red glow of the flickering EXIT sign that hung above the door. The sound of footfalls on the tile floor echoed behind him. He quickened his pace as the sound grew nearer. He took off running. The sound of his helmet clattering to the floor startled him anew. When Delaney turned to pick it up, the hair on the back of his neck stood on end. He thought he heard a soft laugh.

"Fuck it."

He turned back to the exit door. He extended his hands toward the brushed aluminum push-bar. It made a loud click as he pressed against it, the door giving way. As he pushed through the exit, he felt someone's breath on the back of his neck.

It was pitch black as he emerged into the chilly air. The door exited to a void under the stairs leading to Building 1's southern entrance where a set of concrete stairs led to ground level. He took the stairs two at a time, pausing only when he emerged into the silvery light of a full moon. He took a deep breath as he gathered his composure.

"You're being ridiculous," he chided himself. He started fumbling with his keys and turned to go back in and retrieve the abandoned helmet.

The hairs on the back of his neck stood on end and his skin goose-pimpled at a puff of cool air that kissed the back of his neck. He thought he heard something, but it was too soft and quiet. He moved toward the steps into the void. The puff of air caressed his neck again and tickled his ear; this time the voice was louder.

"That wouldn't be a good idea."

He closed his eyes as fear gripped his heart, no longer worried about riding without his brain bucket. He sprinted to his Harley and frantically started it and roared off. He didn't care that in just over 12 hours he would have to explain why he sped through the main gate on a motorcycle without a helmet.

Season One: Episode 20
Gateway to the West and the Beyond

"When I was 10, I started hearing voices. My parents thought I was crazy, so they took me to a psychologist. I told him I was speaking to my grandfather who was telling me about fighting in the Vietnam War. I was talking about things that no one else in the family knew about. When my grandmother reached out to one of his friends, he confirmed everything I was saying was true. I was not crazy. I have a gift, and I use that gift to help people, living and dead, find closure. My name is Dick Fisher, and I am a medium who, with the help of my wife Mary, helps dead people."

"I retired from the FBI where I investigated some of the biggest financial crimes in our nation's recent history. Places, institutions, families, and people have history buried in their closets that they do not want uncovered. I was a skeptic, thinking that mediums were con men. Then I worked with Dick as a crime victim on a case where a pyramid scheme cost him his 401(k). He knew things about the case that the FBI was not releasing to the public. Now we team up helping people across the country find closure for whatever haunts them. My name is Special Agent, Retired, Jackie Bierman, and I investigate the hidden histories of haunted houses."

\- Intro to *Haunted Houses*

Chapter One

Federal Bureau of Investigation Special Agent (retired) Jacquelyn Bierman recorded part of her voiceover for a television show she was doing
with Dick and Mary Fisher. The recording equipment was operated by Dan
Uebel, who doubled as sound recorder and cameraman. Her words would be
dubbed over video of her driving down I-270, turning onto Telegraph Road,
and passing through the somber beauty of the Jefferson Barracks National
Cemetery and St. Louis County Park.

> *"Today we are visiting St. Louis, Missouri, home of Jefferson Barracks, the*
> *oldest U.S. military installation west of the Mississippi. The airmen and sol-*
> *diers stationed there lovingly refer to it as 'JB.' It was established in 1826 and*
> *named after President and Founding Father Thomas Jefferson. We were called*
> *in by Lieutenant Colonel Mickey 'Logan' Delaney, a high-ranking officer in the*
> *Missouri Air National Guard. Over the course of his 15 years of service at the*
> *base, he reports having experienced several encounters with the paranormal."*

The next scene was of her shaking hands with a tall officer in a flight suit standing by a naval gun captured off the Spanish cruiser *Almirante Oquendo* during the Spanish-American War. The mighty Mississippi River rushed through the background, heading south toward the Gulf of Mexico.

"Lieutenant Colonel Delaney, it's a pleasure meeting you. It's always an honor speaking to our country's best and bravest."

"Thank you for your support and your service," Delaney replied.

"Before we get started, military and first responder nicknames have always fascinated me. How did you get the nickname *Logan*?"

Delaney smiled and gave a soft chuckle. "Well, it is a comic book reference for a football reference."

Jackie cocked her head questioningly.

Delaney continued. "I used to play college ball for *the* best state school in the country: *The* Ohio State University. We had a rivalry with the state school to our north. I won't even mention the state's name, but their mascot is the wolverine. Since Logan is the alter-ego of the superhero Wolverine, people thought it would be funny to make that my callsign."

"All right," Jackie said, "now you said that you have experienced some supernatural occurrences on base?"

"Yes, ma'am. I was single and just started working at the unit full-time, hired directly from active duty. I did not have a place to stay just yet, so I had a cot set up in my office. The sound of these heavy doors opening and closing over by the breakroom would wake me up. The first couple of times I went to go check and no one was there. What's more, the lights were off when I got near them."

"Did someone not turn on the hall lights as they snuck around?"

"Nope. The lights are motion-activated, so if someone had opened them, the lights would have been on."

"Anything else?"

"I would hear people walking around when I *knew* I was the only person in the building. Needless to say, I decided to speed up my house hunting."

"Are you the only one in your unit to experience anything paranormal?"

The officer laughed. "Oh no. I have a sergeant who once was sitting at his corner computer station, the only person in the room. He said he heard the sound of a cubicle's overhead bin door being opened and then clattering closed as if dropped. He turned to see who else was in the room with him when he heard his CAC card being lifted—" Logan paused before continuing. "Oh, sorry, I mean our ID cards that we use to log into our computers. Sometimes I forget to translate into civilian! Anyway, it sounded as if it were lifted out of the reader and reinserted. He swung back to his screen and saw that he had been logged out of his computer."

"What did he do?"

Delaney laughed again. "Well, he got up as quickly as he could and went to the master sergeant who had an office next to mine. I heard him telling his story and stepped over to tell him mine. But we're not the only ones. If you randomly pick out 10 guardsmen stationed here, five or six will have ghost stories of their own. There is another lieutenant colonel who once saw a Confederate general working late at night at Building 1."

"So, are these the places we'll be visiting?"

Delaney shook his head. "Unfortunately, those are actively in use so Mr. Fisher will not be allowed in those. However, there are a few buildings that are not currently in use by either the Air or Army Guard, so he will be given access there."

"Have you ever had any experiences there?"

"I have not had many experiences outside of my own building." He put his hands on his hips and stared across the base as he thought about where to begin.

"There are stories for most of the buildings. For example, there's Building 78 which we call the White Elephant because it is the largest building on base, and it is painted white and not the red brick of the rest of the base's buildings. A few of the Army's guardsmen have stayed there from time to time. Many claimed to see things, but it's been empty for the past few years.

"There's also Building 28. It used to be a barracks for the men who were stationed here. Your night crew will have access since it is empty, having been closed for over a decade."

"Do you know of anything that has ever happened at Building 28?"

"In the early '80s, there were some NCOs—sergeants—leaving after working late. The chief master sergeant in the group noticed a light was on up on the third floor. He sent the lowest ranking NCO to run upstairs and turn off the light. The guy ran upstairs and turned it off. When he came back down, the light was on again. I think they sent this guy upstairs like three times before they decided to just leave."

"Was the light back on when they left?"

"According to the story, no one looked back. But also, the original JB was 1,600 or 1,700 acres. Now the base sits on less than 200 acres. Over time, the base was partitioned into the National Cemetery and Veterans Administration hospital. After World War II, the base was deactivated from active-duty service and turned over to the Missouri Air National Guard. We were cut down to our current size at that time, and the rest of the land was turned over to the St. Louis County parks department. The theater became a Catholic church, and the hospital was converted into use by a school district."

"Wow, a lot of history here," Jackie observed.

Chapter Two

Tonight had gone well for Jared Pucket, the cameraman for Dick and Mary Fisher. Usually, he would have to leapfrog the show's stars as they drove to the shooting location, but tonight he had an assistant.

Senior Airman Jeremy Dunn had volunteered to help with the filming. The airman thought he was going to be shooting video all night. His mood soured when he found out he would only be helping capture the drive to the Air National Guard Station. After that, he was just there to provide escort— to be a babysitter.

It was night when Dick and Mary arrived at JB. The final shot happened when the couple pulled into the main gate of the base. Unlike Dan who remained in the background, Jared had an important role to play in the show. He made sure there were not any objects that would indicate who inhabited the buildings currently or in the past. He also sought to hide clues that would indicate the function of the buildings; this gave Dick's description of his interactions with the spirits more credibility. Jared would set up a camera to show him doing this, making him a minor part of the show. After this, as Dan did for Jackie, he would record Dick's voiceover.

> *"I have no contact with Jackie until after the investigation is over. This way I cannot be influenced by the things she uncovers. Before I do, Jared usually precedes me and cleanses the place of any personal effects that could give me clues as to who lives here. He got lucky today and did not have to do any cleaning. From what we were told, the buildings should be empty due to renovations taking place. The first building we are going to is Building 78, which is lovingly called the White Elephant by the soldiers stationed at Jefferson Barracks, often simply called JB."*

The voiceover ended with their rental car pulling up to the building. Airman Dunn, having told Jared there was nothing of value to guard in the building, opted to stay in his car.

Mary, armed with a small camcorder, got out and recorded her husband exiting the vehicle. The footage would be spliced in post-production for maximum dramatic effect. The medium held a flashlight in one hand.

> *"My wife, Mary, accompanies me on the walk. She helps me focus and silence all the background energy that could interfere."*

Dick walked around a staircase leading up to double doors.

"This is not good," he said, shaking his head. "Something bad happened here. I can sense their despair."

He headed up the stairs and tried the double doors. They opened for him, and he entered the dark building. He turned on the flashlight to see through the darkness, as all power to the building had long been cut. The beam sliced across the abandoned space, catching the movement of a mouse scurrying across the baseboards at the far end of the foyer. To his left, he could see the remains of a kitchen and a lounge. Furniture from the 1980s or earlier was rotting, torn apart by various rodents searching for nest-building materials.

"I don't sense anything up here, but we are close. Like something bad happened *above* us."

He took off, searching for a staircase leading to the next floor. He spotted it in a windowless hallway. They wound their way to the third floor. Dick headed straight to a door that would be difficult to see if one were not specifically looking for it.

"Here. Whatever it was . . . happened here." He opened it, the empty space was about the size of a large closet. Dick's gaze drifted to the ceiling. "No one knew this room was here for a while. Someone died in here, but no one knew right away. It took weeks . . . maybe months to find the body."

"Was the person murdered?" Mary asked, her uncanny sense of when it was okay to interrupt with questions having been perfected after years of marriage.

On the other hand, Jared just filmed, knowing not to speak and to be as quiet as possible. This made him the perfect cameraman for Dick's walks. For the first episode, the producer had sent a guy named Ramsey who had a habit of talking almost incessantly during the shoot. He was let go and Liz, Jared's wife and the show's make-up artist, asked if they would give Jared a shot. Fortunately for all, Jared proved worthy.

Despite his discipline at remaining quiet, Jared thought of speaking up now. On the first walk he filmed, he felt a tingle at the back of his neck that caused the hair to stand right up. Dick had led them to a place where he had a powerful vision. Jared did not feel that sensation on all the walks he filmed, but he was experiencing it now.

Dick tapped his chin in thought as Mary's question about a possible murder hung in the air. "I don't think so. I see rope and feel . . . despair. He— I'm pretty sure it was a guy—could have been murdered, but I think he more than likely killed himself." He walked into the space, looking at the walls.

Jared shivered, feeling like someone was watching him.

Dick was too far in his trancelike state to take notice of his cameraman's slight tremble. "He had secrets like this room. He must have been someone in charge. An architect? The contractor?" He looked back over his shoulder at

Mary and Jared as they filmed him. "There is just overwhelming sadness here. I think they walled it up after finding him here. But someone else used it."

"For what?" Mary asked.

"I don't know. There are papers . . . like records. Books scattered about and photos. Old-timey photos."

As Dick and Mary talked, Jared saw something out of the corner of his eye. It was a dark figure, and he did his best to dismiss it as a trick of shadow until it moved, only to then fade into nothingness. Instinctively, he jerked his camera to point at the now empty space.

At the same moment, Dick's gaze snapped to where the figure had been standing. "Jared, what is it? Did you see something?" Dick's voice was calm and collected, knowing the answer before asking the question.

Jared blushed. "Aw, I don't know. I thought I did." He was a little embarrassed, thinking he could be wrong. "I thought I saw a shadowy figure, like it was watching us. I was trying to ignore it because I thought it was a shadow from our lights . . . until it moved."

Dick stepped toward the cameraman and looked at him for a moment before placing a hand on his shoulder. "It very well could have been," he said, a reassuring tone in his voice.

Chapter Three

Jackie's rental weaved its way through downtown traffic toward Saint Louis University. The route was longer than necessary in order to showcase the city's parks, gentrified neighborhoods, and the efforts of the university to revitalize the area around campus; the university did not want to highlight the urban blight surrounding the campus to prospective donors and parents. Later in the studio, the editor would splice her voiceover onto the footage Dan had shot.

> *"Normally I would speak to other people who lived, or in this case worked, in the building we are investigating. However, that is not the case here, given the sensitivity of being in the military and the subject matter being something few people were willing to talk about publicly for a TV show.*
>
> *"However, we lucked out. Military installations are fertile grounds for ghost stories and hauntings for a paranormal investigator to study Lieutenant Colonel Delaney provided us with enough stories that he had*

collected through the years so that we could jump straight to the experts.

"So, today I am traveling to Saint Louis University, or SLU, to speak with Doctor James Simokaitis. He is a professor of American history specializing in the frontier and westward expansion. Those who run the museums around the base all mentioned his name as the foremost expert on the history of JB and the surrounding area."

Jackie entered Chouteau Hall after parking at a meter and hiking a block to the campus. She navigated her way to the professor's office and knocked on the door.

"Come in!" The voice from the other side was friendly and inviting.

She pushed the door open, and a gentleman in his early sixties stood up and took off his reading glasses. He wore a tweed jacket, a dress shirt with the top button unfastened, and a pair of Dockers. He had the business casual look of a liberal arts professor who came of age in the '80s.

"Special Agent, Retired, Bierman, I assume?" He half bowed with a mischievous yet charming smile on his face.

"Professor Simokaitis, I presume?" she asked, extending her hand which he shook.

"Yes, yes. Please, just call me Simo. No reason for all the formality stuff. You said you wanted to talk to me about JB and the hauntings there? Hm?"

"Yes. I spoke to Lieutenant Colonel Delaney—"

"I know him," he said, his tone flat and unreadable.

"He spoke about some experiences he had on the base, seeing things. He also spoke about things other soldiers saw—"

"Airmen. Soldiers are Army, Delaney is Air Force." His chiding was friendly, but it was still a correction. "They get touchy when you confuse one for another."

"He said there was a long history of hauntings at the place," she pressed on. "Perhaps you could shed some light on events that could have led people to stick around after shedding the mortal coil?"

He leaned back in his desk chair, collecting his thoughts. "Well, there is plenty of drama centered around Jefferson Barracks. It was the first military base established in the West. St. Louis was a jumping-off point for westward expansion, and for about a century was one of, if not *the*, most important forts in the U.S. It was a POW prison for Confederates, Nazis, and the Japanese. It was the birthplace of cavalry and an early training base for the Army Air Corps. In 1890, they started to modernize the base; by the end of that decade, all the primitive limestone structures were torn down and replaced by red brick buildings."

"So those are the broad brushes of the history of the place. What about specific incidents?" As she interrupted with her question, she made a show of taking notes for the camera.

"That's one of the problems. So many people have passed through the old North Gate that there are plenty of stories. There's a cemetery there. How many people are buried there because they died in the Spanish Flu epidemic in 1918? Or other disease outbreaks? These are legends shrouded in mystery. My favorite one is the haunting of the White Elephant."

"White Elephant?"

"Yes, otherwise known as Atkinson Hall or Building 78. It was built in 1912 as a chow hall. At its height, it could feed thousands. Some of the officers in charge have placed the number between 1,600-4,000 troops at one time. Anyway, there is a room on the third floor that, rumor has it, the contractor who built the facility committed suicide in."

"So, you are familiar with the base's ghost stories?"

He nodded. "It is kind of hard to miss. St. Louis has a long history. As American cities go, a lot has happened here. Including the real exorcism that the movie was based on."

Jackie's interest was piqued. She knew she should stay on topic and steer the conversation toward Jefferson Barracks, but the morsel of the real exorcism was too much red meat to leave unexplored. "You mean the girl—"

"It was actually a boy from the Northeast. He was Lutheran, and members of his family were into the Spiritualism movement and regularly tried communicating with the dead. Weird things began happening, all centered on the boy." His eyes got big, and his cordial tone got even more excited. "The family pastor attempted an exorcism but was untrained in the ritual. Reportedly, he got his ass kicked and refused to help anymore. The boy had family in this area, a cousin or someone was going to Saint Louis University for nursing. She said she would speak to one of the Jesuit priests here, and one who was a trained exorcist agreed. The boy came and lived in St. Louis for a while. After being rid of the demon, he converted to Catholicism."

"Do you know why the character was a girl in the movie?"

"William Peter Blatty wrote about it after hearing the story at Georgetown, which is why he changed the city from humble St. Louis to D.C. He may have changed the gender to protect the identity of the kid who wanted to remain anonymous."

"When did this happen?"

"1949. The boy lived with his family or at a hospital that was torn down a couple of decades ago. Although he did meet with Father Bowdern at the college's church." He indicated the direction with his eyes.

Jackie shook off her uneasiness at the story of the historical events behind *The Exorcist*. "Well . . . back to the White Elephant. Do you have any pictures or information about the man who committed suicide in that room?"

"Unfortunately, no. There is nothing to corroborate the stories; that said there is nothing to *disprove* them either. In the absence of truth, at some point in history, the stories take on a life of their own." He shrugged his shoulders in exasperated defeat. "Now I do know the Army has allowed some of its soldiers to live in the building from time to time if they are down on their luck. From what I have heard from my friends serving there, stories of hearing someone, or *something*, moving about are common. As are reports of shadowy figures who appear to be watching the temporary residents."

Chapter Four

Dick's voice was dubbed over images of him, Mary, and Airman Dunn getting in their cars to head to the next building.

> "On post, we were only allowed access to Atkinson Hall and Building 28 because they were empty, and we were not deemed a security risk in buildings that were going to be completely renovated into office space. We were accompanied by an airman who was very good at keeping his distance so as to not interrupt my trance. As I approached Building 28, it just felt like a barracks. It looked like where you would expect the Army to house groups of soldiers who would then share their space and their lives with one another. The sense of camaraderie and drama that comes with such a lifestyle hit me the moment I stepped foot in the door."

"So many have lived in this building," Dick said as he stepped inside. To his left and right were open bays where bunk beds once lined the walls for men trained to go fight in Cuba, Europe, and the Pacific. "So many people, mostly men, passed through here. They are whispering. It is hard to make out any one voice. Perhaps if we got higher?"

Airman Dunn, following at a distance, was visibly uncomfortable being in the building after dark. He had refused to go into Building 78 with the crew, opting to stay outside by Dick and Jared's rental vehicles. However, this building was in the beginning stages of renovation, and the workers had left tools behind that needed to be safeguarded.

As they started the final flight up to the third floor, they noticed a light glowing meekly against the dark.

"It's quieter up here. The voices on the first two floors are still here, but they're muted," Dick said as Mary focused her camcorder on him. "Still, we are not entirely alone."

The third floor consisted of an anteroom serving two empty conference rooms. In it was the source of the light they had seen coming upstairs— a work light carelessly left on. The medium walked from the empty room on his left to the empty room on the other side of the third-floor foyer.

"It is important that we know this building is haunted. I see a man, close-cropped hair. He has five . . . six stripes on his sleeves. He died in this building, suddenly, but not up here . . . and not the way that people think. He wants me to check out the basement." Dick moved with purpose out of the room and toward the stairs.

Airman Dunn was milling about the anteroom as the group started moving downstairs. He stepped over to the work light the contractors had left on and flipped the switch. The room fell into darkness, which did not suit him, so he hurried after the group.

They made their way down to the basement. It smelled slightly of dampness and history. Light from the flashlights carried by Dick and Airman Dunn, reinforced by Mary's and Jared's camera lights, splashed across the walls and floor, putting the 1890s construction methods on full display. In a few places, they even found ancient electrical wiring complete with paper insulation.

Directly three stories down from where Dick spoke with the spirit, they entered a large room. As they moved deeper into the darkness, the temperature got remarkably colder.

"I have a bad feeling about this," Dick stated, coming to a full stop inside the cold spot.

The airman had stopped in the doorway—a primal survival instinct preventing him from entering the room.

Jared felt the hair on the back of his neck rise once more. He was starting to decide he did not like this base. He felt relieved when his camera's light revealed an exterior door not 10 feet from them.

"It was here. In this spot where the soldier—no, not a soldier," he paused, "Air Force . . . died. It looked like natural causes, but it wasn't. It was . . . evil. Vengeful. Dead. Something down here does not like the military."

At first, Airman Dunn thought the movement was a trick of light and shadow. There was no possible way the hazy figure *really* existed; it was the power of suggestion using his own eyes to fool him. The form stalking toward him with purpose and moving like smoke was just a figment of his imagination. Nonetheless, he froze, his heart pounding in his chest. His mouth opened to speak, but no words escaped his lips. Tears slid down his cheeks. He shook his head as the figure started to develop recognizably human features.

For the crew, not paying attention to the airman, the room suddenly got noticeably warmer.

"It was here. The entity that killed the airman upstairs. But it's gone now," Dick observed.

The shadow had manifested itself behind them. It was wearing a black uniform. A skull and crossbones adorned the peaked hat the terrible visage wore. Its blue eyes burned with hatred as it reached for Airman Dunn with skeletal hands. He pressed his back against the door and fumbled for the doorknob. The creature's human character suddenly disintegrated in front of him, leaving a black-eyed skull with its jaw hanging open as if to consume the young man's very essence. As his hand found the doorknob and turned it, his throat found its voice. A shrill scream escaped as he fled through the door.

The crew turned, catching a brief shot of the airman disappearing through the open door into the blackness on the other side. They all noticed that the air between them and their escort seemed to have a hazy quality to it.

"Guys, I'm sorry to interrupt, but can we go out this door?" Jared said, ready to end the shoot and leave without passing through the dark, stagnant fog now standing between them and the way they had just come.

"I think that would be okay," Dick said as Mary nodded in agreement. This time, he was not the least bit upset with the cameraman for interrupting his trance.

* * *

The exit Jared had found opened to an alley behind the building that was built into a hill. This meant the walk to their cars was a slight uphill trek, but it did not bother them in the least. All were happy to be out of the building and away from whatever inhabited the basement.

They found Airman Dunn curled up in front of his car across the street in front of Building 28. He was trembling.

"If it is okay with you guys, I think I'm going to go home now. The next part of your walk is in the park. That's no longer military so . . . yeah. I'm going home. You don't need me anymore." He stood and walked to the driver's side of his beaten-up compact.

Jared's voice made him pause. "Hey, goodnight and thanks. Didn't you turn off the light on the third floor?"

The airman turned around and looked up. His gaze followed Jared's extended arm to the middle windows of the foyer. The third-floor window was lit by the soft glow of a work light. Shaking his head, Airman Dunn slid into the driver's seat of his car and drove away.

Chapter Five

"This was an unusual episode for me. Usually, I would attempt to set up several meetings with local experts such as the police chief, other first responders, medical examiners, or anyone else with the credentials to shed light on the property we are looking into. But Jefferson Barracks is different. It is not just one building, but many. Some are on a military base, and the rest are either in a public park or in private hands. So, I only needed to talk to two people: Professor Simo and Major, Retired, Darryl Goodman."

"You mentioned Atkinson Hall. That is one of the buildings we are allowed in because it is empty at the moment."

"Interesting," Simo said, leaning across his desk. "What are the other ones?"

"Well, there is only one other one on the base itself. It does not have a name, just Building 28. Then the last one is the Old Powder Magazine located in the park. We set up a walk there with the county."

"Building 28, you say?" He leaned back in his chair, tapping his glasses on his desktop. "Interesting. There was a death there in the 1960s. A master sergeant was working late after a drill on a Sunday down in the basement. He was a little older, in his late forties, and he had a heart attack. The full-timers found him the next day. His name was Master Sergeant Eric Hale. I kinda figured they would limit you to unused buildings, so I went ahead and found the obituary from the *St. Louis Post-Dispatch*. It had his picture, so I printed it out if that helps."

He slid the picture across the table toward Jackie. She studied it for a moment. He had been a handsome man, and if he were a little younger, he would have been a poster boy for the Air National Guard or the Air Force. Fit with close-cropped hair, the man fit the ideal of every recruitment poster she had ever seen.

"Do you know anything special about Building 28?" she asked hopefully, looking up from the printout.

"It was a barracks at one point, serving as quarters for the men mustering there to ship out to the Spanish-American War or World War I. I'm not sure if it, like all the buildings numbered 26 through 29, housed trainees assigned there for basic or technical training for the Army Air Corps."

"Who else would it have housed?"

"Germans. Japanese. Prisoners of war were shipped back to the U.S., putting an ocean between them and whatever front they had fought on. Some were sent here to St. Louis. If the Germans behaved, they were even allowed off-base passes. Many stayed after the war, having taken local brides in the ethnically German community."

"Really? Americans marrying Nazis?"

"Not all Germans were Nazis. Hitler came in second in the 1932 election with only about 36% of the vote. He was able to consolidate power only because the Nazis were the largest party among many. Once in control of the Reichstag, he was able to maneuver himself so he could take power when Hindenburg, who won in '32, died in '34. Most of the guys sent here were apolitical troops, unaware of the excesses of their leaders. It was not until later in the war, after it was essentially over, that we caught the people responsible for the true evil. The guys here mostly were not Gestapo or SS. The ones allowed off-base liberty were not the few actual Nazis who were imprisoned here."

"Did they keep the Nazi true believers in Building 28?"

"Not necessarily. However, prisoners were employed across the base doing various jobs that needed to be done. Everything from janitorial duties to skilled labor jobs like electricians or plumbers."

Interlude

SS-Obersturmführer Wolfgang Bader was working, unsupervised, in the basement of Building 28. He was applying his knowledge of electrical engineering to work as an electrician. When he was captured by the Americans, he was wearing the uniform of a feldwebel, the German Army's equivalent to a sergeant or staff sergeant in the U.S. Army. Fearing a schutzstaffel, or SS, officer would be mistreated, he told his captors he was a humble electrician drafted into a war he did not want.

The Americans asked him to renounce the Führer and the Nazis, which he did. He explained his SS blood tattoo resulted from being treated in an SS hospital, where it was standard practice for medics to give the tattoo to the non-SS military under their care. He passed muster and eventually ended up in St. Louis, which proved comfortable. He performed his work well, taking pride in it, and found himself rewarded regularly with off-base passes. He started going to a German Catholic church where he met and soon started dating a third-generation Aryan girl.

It was difficult at first. Many of the congregants had sons fighting in Europe and did not approve of German prisoners of war dating their daughters who were now more American than German. It was difficult for men like Wolfgang, but not impossible.

Adalie Neumann was a pretty blonde woman whom he was planning to marry, and he planned to then remain in the United States. It took great effort to convince her family he was a good man and not a Nazi. Eventually, when he asked her father for her hand in marriage, the elder man agreed.

However, his thoughts were not with his beloved today. His captors were celebrating. Hitler was dead, and his captors were passing around copies of the *St. Louis Post-Dispatch* as the news broke in the U.S. They were celebrating the death of the man who had lifted Germany out of the morass following their humiliation at the end of World War I. He feigned happiness, but it wore on him. He threw himself into his work. He was working on the wiring for the structure built at the dawn of electricity by helping replace the paper-clad wiring.

He heard the door open and glanced over his shoulder to see corporal Levi Schwartz of the base military police, or MPs, enter. "Corporal Schwartz—"

"You fuckin' Kraut, SS son of a bitch!" the corporal yelled, his voice booming in the partially subterranean room. The man was *very* pissed. "You fucking liar!"

"What did I lie about?" Wolfgang asked, palming a razor knife behind his back.

"Everything. *Not* being in the SS. The fucking swastika *you* carved into the retaining wall by the sundial!" Corporal Schwartz yelled.

The accusation made it difficult for the German *not* to smile. He carved the symbol into the stone wall capstone as a sign of anonymous defiance for having to deny his true beliefs.

"I told you—"

"Shut up! I saw you, but you have the CO wrapped around your finger. He believed *you* over me. But not anymore." The MP stopped about 10 feet from the prisoner, his hand moving down to his holstered Colt .45.

This was it. The SS officer recognized the look of murder in a man's eyes. He had one chance. He was close enough that he could easily beat the MP's draw, so he lunged, wielding the knife from behind his back.

Corporal Schwartz was ready for the attack. As the Nazi rushed him, the MP kicked, landing the blow in his attacker's gut. Wolfgang crumpled over.

Schwartz pulled his .45 and stepped over his victim. "I know. I know you were at the pogroms. I had family there. They spoke of an SS-Obersturmführer Wolfgang Bader. There was a picture of you with my aunt. We know. We know you censored their letters, but we have a code. We knew what they were *really* telling us about. What they were *really* warning us against." He pulled the trigger, placing a round in the other man's abdomen.

"Fucking Jew! Your kind ruined the Fatherland!" Bader cried out in anger. He heard the sound of footsteps on the floor above them, scurrying to respond to the shots fired. "I won't die. They will stop you! They will save me, and you will be court-martialed!"

"Heil Hitler!" SS-Obersturmführer Wolfgang Bader said, extending his right hand in salute. Rage and hatred filled his heart. "Heil Xa—" he started to shout as he saw the flash of the muzzle—the last thing he ever saw.

"You're right," the corporal said softly, strangely calm.

May 7, 1961

It was Sunday after another drill weekend, and Master Sergeant Eric Hale was working late, making sure his men got paid. He was also trying to figure out if trying to get promoted to senior master sergeant would be worth it. He was not getting any younger and had been thinking of retiring right before the Military Pay Act of 1958 authorized two new enlisted pay grades.

It would be a decent boost to his retirement. He had been active throughout World War II and called back for Korea. The Air National Guard

had given him a chance to finish his military career at home at the McDon-
nell Aircraft Corporation factory in North St. Louis building jet fighters. He
was tired and wanted to be able to go home to his wife and enjoy her com-
pany a little bit before going to bed and getting up early for work.

His body was aching. In World War II, he served as a ball gunner on
B-17s over Europe. Master Sergeant Hale had received two Purple Hearts as a
Flying Fortress crew member. In Korea, he was a tail gunner in a B-29 Superfor-
tress. On a ferry flight from the United States to Japan, his aircraft crashed in
a rice paddy. He had been knocked unconscious as his forehead bounced
off the sight.

The flight engineer, who was also injured in the accident, ran to the
back of the burning aircraft to pull his comrade out of the smoldering hunk
of metal. That man was on the fast track to sew on chief master sergeant,
and Hale could think of no man better for the new rank. He thought about
giving Leo a call as he shuffled paperwork.

The master sergeant signed the last pay document and put it in the envelope to give to the pay clerk. He left his basement office to drop it off in the
squadron clerk's office and then go home. He shivered as he passed through
a cold spot. The NCO paused to listen for the HVAC; he could not hear it.

He suddenly felt something on the back of his neck, like someone's cold
hand. As the hairs on the back of Hale's neck stood on end, he turned around
and came face-to-face with a translucent human figure in a black SS uniform.
A skull peered at him with black, soulless eyes beneath a black peaked hat,
complete with the iconic skull and crossbones.

Master Sergeant Hale gripped his chest as he felt his heart stop.

Chapter Six

In order to get some night shots of them driving, Dick and Mary followed behind Jared on the drive to the next building. Outside the fence line of the Jefferson Barracks Air National Guard Station, much of the original base had been turned over to St. Louis County to become a park. Many buildings were converted from military use to schools, Catholic churches, or several museums. The Old Powder Magazine was one of the museums and was not far. However, since they needed footage for Dick's voiceover, the short trip was stretched out.

> *"After Airman Dunn left, we headed over to the Old Powder Magazine. Normally, my walks are less restricted, but since we are investigating a military base and public property, we had to get permission to be here at night and access buildings that would normally be closed. This meant that I could not necessarily go where my guides would normally tell me to go."*

The Old Powder Magazine was a nondescript, gray stone building surrounded by a fence made of the same material as the structure it guarded. A county park ranger had opened the museum and turned on the lights for the TV crew. Dick led the group inside but only stayed there for about five minutes or so.

"I don't think there is much going on *inside* the building. However, there is someone outside the building." He led his wife and Jared around the outside of the fence. "Someone *is* guarding this place. He feels it is his duty to remain here. To remain vigilant." He stepped away from the building and toward the woodline. "I see a man. He is wearing a Civil War uniform."

"North or South?" Mary asked.

"North. He's Union and very proud of it." Dick stopped near what could have been a game trail for the numerous deer infesting the park. "I can sense he feels concern for a fallen comrade. He may also feel a little betrayed."

"Was there a battle here?"

He shook his head in answer. "Not a battle but ... violence. Like a murder or assassination. No—he was not a big enough target to be the victim of an assassination. He was targeted as part of a raid."

Chapter Seven

Sometimes Dan helped book guests for the show. Today he made arrangements for a meeting with Major (Retired) Darryl Goodman at Café Telegraph, a popular restaurant just outside Jefferson Barracks Park. He arrived before Jackie and the retired soldier to set up the camera and sound equipment in the room used for group events. He sat quietly and waited for the star and her interviewee to arrive.

> *"Today I'm meeting with a retired officer from the Army Reserve unit on JB. His name is Darryl Goodman and, as a major, he commanded troops in Afghanistan following 9-11. He has a Master's degree in military history and has specialized in the military history of St. Louis. He is also a paranormal investigator for a local group of ghost hunters called the Midwest Paranormal Investigative Society. Darryl has published a book about the haunted history of Jefferson Barracks called* The Spirits of Jefferson Barracks.*"*

Dan looked up when he heard Jackie's voice and her heels clicking on the cement floor.

"Hi Dan, is Darryl here yet?"

"Nope." Dan was a man of few words. He stroked his goatee as he tended to his camera equipment.

Jackie went to work setting up for her interview with the retired major. Focused on her notes, she missed him sneaking up behind her.

"Hello, Agent Bierman," a male voice greeted her from behind.

She startled a little and stood up. "Yes, sir." She extended her hand and a smile.

"It is good to meet you. I hear you want to talk about ghosts at JB."

"Yes. Dan, are we recording?"

He gave her a thumbs-up.

"We are recording. Do you prefer Mr. or Major Goodman?"

He laughed. "Just call me Darryl. Is there a particular ghost you want to talk about?" He turned the tables on her as he turned the interview into a conversation.

"Yes, actually." She found herself at ease with his conversational tone. "The sentry at the Old Powder Magazine."

"That is an interesting case and one that is more legend than verified history. So please take what I say with a grain of salt. Some of it is my personal theory and conjecture. Going back to Missouri during the Civil War, it was a slave state that trended toward supporting the Confederacy. In fact, Lincoln marched a sizable force into the state to occupy it and keep it in the Union. There were several battles with some of the progenitors of the Missouri National Guard.

"Here in St. Louis, you had this enclave of Germans who actually held loyalty to the U.S. and not the CSA. It was an important naval chokepoint—"

"*Naval* chokepoint?" she interrupted. "Missouri is landlocked. What would have been its naval importance?"

"Because of the Mississippi River. The Confederates were running smuggling operations up and down the old muddy river since it was, and is, a significant waterway. So much so that the state organized a Naval Militia in 1902. It saw action in World War I. So, think of it as a brown-water navy."

"Brown water?"

"Same thing as saying river. The Confederates were interested in raiding JB for arms and munitions stored there. They would picnic close to the fence to make observations about what was going on inside the base, looking for weaknesses in the perimeter and perhaps locating the best places to raid. For a beleaguered force with limited access to arms and munitions, the best target would be the Old Powder Magazine.

"From what I've read, the commanding officer decided to double security. Also, Missouri was a divided state. Southerners were settling the rural areas to spread slavery. However, the St. Louis region was a heavily German area, and they tended to be very pro-Union. So, legend has it a corporal and private were on patrol, and the corporal was a German who was held in high regard. He was paired with a private who was less trustworthy. A raiding party chose their shift to attack, at the end of which the corporal was dead from a shot between the eyes."

"What about the private?"

"He was found unconscious. It looked like someone hit him with the butt of a rifle. He claimed he stepped to the woods to relieve himself and that the next thing he remembered was waking up to his fellow Union soldiers responding to the sound of the gunshot that left his partner dead."

"Do you believe the private's story?"

Darryl shrugged. "It's hard to tell. I have no reason to believe either way. The evidence just does not exist for either his innocence or guilt."

"Is that it? The end of the story?"

"Nope. Fast forward to World War II. The U.S. is using JB as a training base and storing munitions here, so you have heightened base security. Some of the sentries started claiming they were seeing a Civil War soldier over by the Old Powder Magazine. It got so bad that it soon became a discipline issue. Some soldiers were refusing to patrol at night, even under threat of punishment. In one case, a Private Sean Dunn went absent without leave.

He dropped his rifle, stripped off his jacket, and, by some accounts, he shit—oops, sorry. I mean by some accounts he, uh, pooped himself. They found him at his mother's house not far from the base.

"They brought him back to the base, and he was found mentally incompetent at his court-martial. They gave him a medical discharge."

"How many ghosts do you think are at JB?"

He laughed. "Lots. There was a duel right outside the gate to the Old Powder Magazine. Allegedly, people see the ghosts of one of the duelists there. In the parade field, a woman in white can be seen looking for her lover or a lost child. In the cemetery, there are women looking for dead children. One soldier has been seen standing before two graves, pointing to one and then the other while mouthing words that cannot be heard."

"Wow. What is he doing? Was he buried in the wrong grave?"

"No one really knows." He shrugged again.

"Any other good stories?"

"Well, since you mentioned you were called in by an Air Force officer, this next story is appropriate. In the 1980s, three Air National Guard NCOs were leaving Building 28 after working late into the evening and noticed the light on the third floor was left on. They sent the lowest-ranking guy up there *three* times to turn it off. Each time he claimed he turned the light off, but by the time he got back to his comrades, the light was still on."

"You mentioned that you are a paranormal investigator. What do you think was going on?"

Darryl paused and stared into space, considering the question and all the potential answers. "Well, we're talking about places where people congregate. There are good times and bad. Happiness and sadness. All of this leaves energy behind. The more people, the more residual energy. Military bases tend to attract this sort of energy. People come to them to learn to kill; in many cases, they *do* kill there.

"You also have people from all over coming to one place and bringing their illnesses. I remember basic training. One day I am here in Missouri, the next day I am at Fort Jackson, South Carolina, surrounded by people from every state. One gentleman was from England, another from Puerto Rico. All of us with germs that are normal to ourselves but totally alien to the guys in the bunks on either side of us. Now imagine someone bringing something lethal at a time when medicine is primitive and unable to counter something like the Spanish Flu or an outbreak of consumption."

"Is that why some ghosts are just noises or faded images and others are fully formed like the German corporal?"

"Kind of. In some cases, you have pieces of the person left behind. Other times, they leave behind a more complete version of themselves. These are the so-called intelligent hauntings—the ones that interact with people."

Interlude II

Old Powder Magazine, Jefferson Barracks, Missouri
September 16, 1862

Corporal Herman König was on the night patrol; he was a local boy who, like most Germans but unlike the rest of the state, opposed the Confederacy. The soldier's parents were Bavarian immigrants, and the family felt a strong sense of loyalty to their new home. When the call went out for volunteers, Herman answered.

As the first military installation established west of the Mississippi River, Jefferson Barracks was proving vital to the war effort. While the Union Army built up hospital facilities and shipped in Confederate prisoners, they had also used the location to stockpile arms and munitions. The corporal's mission tonight was to guard the arsenal against Confederate raiders. They had been observed attempting to smuggle arms and supplies down the Mississippi and past the blockade set up at the post overlooking the muddy river.

His commander was nervous. Suspicious-looking picnickers had begun taking lunch outside the perimeter; groups of mostly men had taken to leisurely lunching on the slopes between the base and the riverbanks. The concern was that these individuals were taking note of base defenses and response times. As a precaution, the guard had been doubled.

Corporal König had been paired with Private Patrick Keane. Something about him had not sat well with Herman or his sergeant; while the Irishman had sworn loyalty to the Union, he had been asking questions about where the weak spots in their defenses were.

The private claimed that he was asking so he could better defend the base. This diligence did not extend to his other duties, and so he was always paired with someone whose loyalties were beyond reproach. The redhead was only out of the German's sight when one of them answered the call of nature. As it neared the end of their watch, the private excused himself.

"You about done, Private?" König asked, thinking it was taking the kid too long to take a piss.

When he received no answer, he stepped toward the woodline where his partner had disappeared. By the moonlight filtered through the leaves, he saw a body lying on the ground. A shadowy figure moved through the trees. He shouldered his 1842 Springfield, pointing it into the inky black of the woods. "Identify yourself! Surrender!"

The German's shouted command was answered by a flash of light— seen by his eyes but not registered by his mind—and a thunderclap he never heard.

Old Powder Magazine, Jefferson Barracks, Missouri September 16, 1942

Private Sean Dunn was near the end of his patrol. His commander was concerned that German agents could have infiltrated the heavily German population of St. Louis, so he had doubled the patrols. They had even been equipped with the lightweight M1 Carbine that would have normally only been given to officers or select NCOs. Private Dunn, a slight man, appreciated the lightweight new rifle.

He lit a cigarette—a bad habit he had picked up since joining the Army. His mother had warned him about picking up vices like smoking, alcohol, and women. He had found that he was terrified of women and drinking made him puke, but cigarettes kept him calm and centered. He took a drag, inhaling deep into his lungs while he closed his eyes. The nicotine took its effect on his body. He opened his eyes and saw a human shape illuminated by the full moon.

He shouldered his weapon. "Halt! Identify yourself!" he shouted in a warbling tone.

The form ignored his command, advancing on the sentry.

"I said halt!" he shouted again, charging his weapon. "I *will* shoot you!" He deepened his voice, unsure whether he was attempting to convince the intruder or himself. Most likely he was trying to convince them both.

The man got closer, finally becoming visible. He wore a blue uniform like the Union soldiers in the history books. The man's lips were moving, issuing his own silent challenges to long-dead Confederate raiders. Blood oozed from a .69" hole in his forehead just above the bridge of his nose. Moonlight filtered through the wound, letting Private Dunn see the gore of dripping brain tissue in the murdered soldier's skull.

Private Dunn dropped his rifle, his bowels released, and he took off running in the opposite direction. He ran straight toward a break in the fence that soldiers used to sneak off base to meet up with girlfriends. An hour later his relief found the dropped rifle, and a search found the jacket he had discarded as he ran. Three weeks later, MPs found him hiding out in his mother's house; they had to physically carry the AWOL soldier out of his house, whimpering and begging not to go back to Jefferson Barracks.

Chapter Eight

Dick entered a conference room set aside for him by Lieutenant Colonel Delaney. A sketch artist from the St. Louis County Police Department who had drilled at Jefferson Barracks as a national guardsman waited for him. He took a seat across the table from the woman. She smiled and picked up a pencil. They made small talk as his voiceover began.

"I work with a sketch artist in order to show the homeowner, in this case the service member, what I have seen. Jackie usually uncovers some photos as well, and it's good to compare notes. We do our individual investigations totally separate from one another. That way we do not contaminate our own findings with what the other has found."

"The first entity I want to draw was in Building 78. My wife never saw him."
"It was a he?" the artist asked.
"I believe so. Jared and I both saw him. He would linger even after

46

you turned to look at him, and only then would he fade away. It was like a shadow. Like those targets that cops and soldiers use for target practice. There was no face. No eyes. No nose. No mouth. Just a black human form."

She sketched furiously. After a few minutes, she turned the paper around. "Does this look like the ghost in the building?"

"Yes."

The artist sealed the drawing in a manila envelope and grabbed another piece of paper. "You said you wanted a drawing of what you saw in the basement of Building 28 as well?"

He nodded. "Yes." He paused until she was ready to start drawing. "He was German. A Nazi specifically, but his skin was gaunt to the point of almost being nonexistent at first. Then he became completely skeletal. He was wearing one of those hats the Nazis wore, um, with bills?" He mimed what he had seen.

"The males at my guard unit call them 'bus driver' hats," she said as she started sketching. She looked up from her drawing to see if that was what he had seen.

He nodded.

A few moments later she showed him the new drawing. "Is this accurate?"

Nodding, Dick said, "It is . . . for one of them. Do you mind doing a sketch of the ghost I spoke to on the third floor? We can keep them in the same envelope though."

"Sure thing," the artist responded.

Chapter Nine

Lieutenant Colonel Delaney pulled a few strings and got permission for the crew to shoot in a conference room on base. This time Liz, Jared, and Dan would all be there too. Liz was there for any needed make-up adjustments, and the two cameramen would work different angles at thesame time. Dan trained his camera on Delaney at the head of the table; he was flanked by the American and Missouri flags. Hung between the flags were the shields of the Air Force and Air National Guard. He stood as Jackie and Dick entered.

"Agent Bierman, Mr. Fisher. Good to see you both again."

"And you too, Colonel Delaney," Jackie replied.

"Thanks for setting up the conference room," Dick added.

"I'm glad I could help." He gestured with a hand for them to take a seat.

Usually, they sat across from the person who called them in, but this time Dick took a seat on the man's right, allowing Jackie to take the seat on Delaney's left.

"So, what did you guys find out?"

"Well, like any military installation, Jefferson Barracks has a long history of both good and bad," Jackie started. "For example, take Building 78—"

"The White Elephant," the officer interrupted her.

Jackie nodded. "Yes. Turns out shortly after it was built, they found the body of the contractor who built it between 1910 and 1915. He killed himself in a secret room that no one knew was there. After finding him, the room was walled off. When it was rediscovered, there were military records, books, and other signs that *someone* had been using it."

"Interesting," Dick said. "Was it on the third floor?"

Jackie nodded. "It was." It still creeped her out when he knew things that she had yet to reveal.

"I was drawn to the third floor and to a strange room that was almost like a closet. While we were there, I felt a presence. Almost as if we were being watched. Not only did I see it, but my cameraman saw it too."

"Saw what?" the Air Force officer asked.

Jackie opened the envelope and pulled out the sketch artist's picture from Building 78. "Wow," she said, looking at it and placing it before their client.

Delaney put on a pair of reading glasses before examining the black and white drawing. It was just a black silhouette of a human, but it sent a chill through him. "You actually saw *this*?" he asked over his glasses.

"Yes. As did my cameraman, Jared."

"Is he psychic?"

"It's not about being psychic." Jackie addressed the question before her co-host could answer. "It's about being a medium, sensitive to the dead that surround us."

Dick smiled at her answer. "My co-host is absolutely correct. It is about being attenuated with the unseen world around us."

Delaney nodded. He was a practical man and not normally prone to flights of fancy, but he had seen enough of the paranormal at JB to question some of his assumptions about the things that go bump in the night. "Okay. I'll admit I just don't know that much about the paranormal. So, is this the contractor deciding to just hang around?" He held up the drawing of the shadow figure.

"Possibly," Dick answered. "A common theme for practically every religion is a life after death. Our. Existence. Does. Not. End. Sometimes people remain because they have things left undone. Other times, they remain because they feel the need to protect someone. This entity is neither of those; this is a silent watcher. He did not speak to me."

"Do they ever tell you anything?" Delaney asked, becoming more curious.

"Yes. Our next spirit, for example, died while performing a duty. It happened suddenly, and he wants to warn us about the threat that took his life."

"When did this happen?" Jackie asked.

"I think it happened around the Civil War. He was on patrol, protecting Union weapons and . . . ammo? Bombs?"

"The more accurate term is *munitions*," the officer corrected.

"Thank you, yes, um, munitions. He wants us to know that a comrade had been assaulted first. He'd stepped away for just a moment, and that's when they were attacked. He knew that his leaders didn't think much of his partner and thought he couldn't be trusted, but he wants people to know that the private was not a traitor—that Confederates attacked the Old Powder Magazine *and* the two of them. He also wants to apologize for failing to do his duty. He . . . he wants to apologize for dying."

Dick looked over at the man sitting to his left and saw a tear sliding down Delaney's cheek.

"So, why is it that this guy seems to have remained so . . . complete?" Delaney asked, his voice quivering just a little with the emotion of the dead soldier's sense of duty caught in his throat.

"Sometimes spirits remain in a state of extreme awareness when they die. Like if this man thought there were raiders present, he would have been hypervigilant. Also, feelings of the people around at the time of someone's death can create tremendous energy that will last long after that person dies. So, if the guard was worried about the motives of a partner patrolling with him when he was attacked or if he found out the partner was a Confederate sympathizer, these feelings would remain."

"Even if he realized that his fellow soldier was not a traitor?" Jackie asked. "Wouldn't that resolve the negative feelings that created this energy?"

"No. He indicated he had his own doubts about the private he was with. So, he has some feelings of guilt and is trying to find peace by setting the record straight."

"How long would this last? Is there something a county parks & rec could do?" Delaney asked.

"Over time, the energy will fade and eventually become nothing. But we are talking longer than centuries or even thousands of years. But there *are* things the living can do. Bringing in a priest or a Reiki master can help the dead find peace and move on."

Delaney turned his attention to the retired FBI agent. "Did you find anything out about the Old Powder Magazine?"

She nodded. "I did, sir. I could not find out much besides that a corporal and private were attacked by Confederate raiders during the war. I was unable to discover their names or find pictures.

"However, I did uncover information on an airman who died on base. The man's name was Master Sergeant Eric Hale. He served here in the 1960s and had a heart attack in the basement of Building 28." She slid a photo across the table for Delaney and Dick to look at.

In response, Dick reached for his manila envelope, opened it, and showed the other two the sketches it held.

"Oh my God!" Jackie exclaimed, seeing the horrific drawing of the Nazi.

Delaney whistled and shook his head in disgust.

"And I think we have a match," Dick said as he held up the second sketch from the envelope and the photo side by side.

Jackie and the lieutenant colonel examined them.

"I think you're right," Delaney said first. "It's a dead ringer. What do you think, Agent Bierman?"

"Agreed. What did you learn about him on the walk?"

"Well, he died in the basement but prefers to stay out of it. There is another spirit down there that he blames for his death—one he thinks is absolute evil."

"That's fascinating because he was not the first person to have been documented as dying in the basement of that building," Jackie added. "In World War II, a German prisoner of war was attacked and killed in the basement. A Jewish soldier stationed here who was upset aboutNazi war crimes assaulted and killed a German prisoner. He claimed the man—a model prisoner actually—was actually SS rather than regular Army."

"I also find that interesting because I met Sergeant Hale on the third floor. He totally avoids the basement because of the evil that exists down there. I believe, hearing what you uncovered, this evil is the Nazi killed down there," Dick finished, indicating the gruesome sketch.

"There was another story of three sergeants who were leaving the building after working late into the night. They noticed a light on up on the third floor. So, they sent the lowest-ranking guy to turn it off not once, not twice, but *three* times," Jackie explained.

"Did it finally go off?" the officer asked.

"Unknown. The professor who told me the story said they left after the third time, without looking back."

Delaney had fallen silent, considering what the show's co-hosts had uncovered. He leaned forward to ask a question that had been itching in the back of his mind. "BLUF—bottom line up front: what can we do? What *should* we do?"

"That is *the* question," Dick began. "These spirits are trapped here. I believe the shadow figure is the contractor who killed himself. He shows himself because he has been forgotten. Having taken his life in a moment of extreme despair, he sees the futility of his action and takes his time to fade as a warning to not do what he did.

"In the case of the Nazi in the basement, he was murdered. He may have been the worst sort of person, but his life was taken without trial. He is angry, and his haunting is about getting revenge. Which is 180 degrees opposite the spirit he killed. He has gone to the highest room of the building and is lighting lights as a warning. He has seen the German's true face, and he wants the world to know about it.

"Finally, the Civil War soldier's issue is two-fold. He died doing his duty, which he is continuing in death because that was the last thing he did in life, and he does not know what else to do. He also wants us to know that his partner was not the traitor that their commanding officer thought he may have been. He wants to set the record straight."

Delaney looked Dick in the eyes. "What you're telling me is we should just let them be?"

"This is where it gets tricky. Often, they have a purpose in their haunting. But we have to keep in mind that they are *trapped* in between this life and the next. I believe we have a responsibility to help them get freed from whatever is binding them to this purgatory. Some people want to keep them around as pets, a conversation piece, or even an attraction in the case of some commercial ventures like hotels or bars. We should be calling in a priest or other person capable of exorcising a location so the souls can find peace."

"But how? How can we do that here?" Delaney asked, thinking about all the bureaucracy involved.

Dick closed his eyes and thought for a moment.

"Well," Jackie interjected as she saw her partner struggle to answer, "my investigation found that St. Louis has a strong Catholic history. I believe you could easily find an exorcist here."

"Well, it is more complicated than that," Dick added. "It has to be done by an ordained priest or higher, and the local bishop has to approve of the exorcism. Luckily, you're talking about a building blessing. It's a little less formal, and there is not a medical evaluation to determine whether or not a person is suffering from a mental illness."

"What about the other thing you mentioned?"

"The Reiki master?" Dick asked, and Delaney nodded yes. "Well, that is a form of alternative medicine that also does exorcisms. It originated in Japan. You will not want to have them here at the same time as the Catholic priest since the Holy See considers the practice demonic."

"Do you think it is?" The officer looked concerned.

"I do not. I've worked with a few masters. It is a lot about chi and life forces. It kind of took off during the New Age movement."

"So, Lieutenant Colonel, are you going to take my partner's advice and get the buildings exorcised?"

"I am not going to say yes or no, as I have to talk to our chaplain and base security manager. Plus, our members are pretty conservative, so the priest may be okay but the Reiki master," he struggled to pronounce the unfamiliar term, "may be an issue for many of our folks. But I for one would like to see these spirits move on and find peace."

Six Month Update

The show's director had supervised the editing of shots of the base, the Old Powder Magazine, and Dick's walk into a video sequence with a voice-over by the medium.

> *"Working with the Archdiocese of St. Louis, the Air National Guard units had these buildings blessed. They told me that the priests could feel the presence of spirits left behind. For the most part, the paranormal activity in these locations has decreased."*

The Tale of Mary Deacon

Part One | The Many Abductions of Mary

Prologue

Travis Deacon and his new bride were making their way to the Lake of the Ozarks for their honeymoon. It had been a joyous wedding in the tiny Missouri town of Laquey. The reception was held in the middle school gymnasium and ended sometime around 10:00 p.m. The couple had snuck out to get on the road to Tan-Tar-A Estates at Osage Beach. He lovingly stroked Carol's long, brown hair as she slept on his lap. He smiled. She had been so excited when they got in the truck and proclaimed she would stay awake for the entire drive. She kept the promise for 20 minutes.

While Carol had turned the radio off because she wanted to talk to her new husband, Travis was talked out from the reception and soon found himself running out of things to say. Eventually, she slid across the bench seat and snuggled up to him. Soon her head was in his lap as she began to snooze. He slowed as he crossed over Highway 133 approaching Crocker, a small town of about 600 that once served the railroad that cut through these parts.

Something was wrong. Normally the town's 50 or so streetlights and a dozen or so storefronts bravely held off the encroaching dark of night. But the lights were not on.

"Hey, Carol," he said, his voice barely above a whisper as he softly tapped her head. "Wake up."

He felt her stir in his lap. He tapped her again and raised his voice a little.

"Carol."

Carol sat up and laid her sleepy head on his shoulder. "What? What's wrong? Are we there yet?" she asked through a drowsy fog.

"We're coming up on Crocker."

"Okay?" She lifted her head from his shoulder and looked around somewhat confused. "I don't see anything. It's dark."

"That's just it. It's *too* dark." He leaned forward and peered out his windshield as if this allowed him to pierce the darkness and fathom any secrets it might hold.

She giggled. "Travis, you're being paranoid," Carol soothed.

She had seen him like this before. Travis, two years her senior, had been drafted into the Marines after graduating. He did a tour in Vietnam and earned two Purple Hearts, the last injury severe enough to send him home with a disability claim. He never talked about his experiences in combat with her. She had seen the scars, both physical and mental, and knew to honor his sacrifice mostly in silence.

He leaned back in his seat. "Yeah, I guess so. There are usually more lights," he paused, "but tonight there are no lights. At all."

She could feel his body tighten, ready to fight or flee at any moment if danger appeared. She teased her hand up his thigh toward the top of his jeans. She playfully traced the line of the zipper, the circle of the button.

"I know what can make you feel better." She smiled as she unbuttoned his pants and put her head back in his lap.

Soon Travis felt the tension release as his muscles relaxed. He caressed her hair as he entered the town. Despite the wonderful sensations of her mouth, his mind could not completely ignore the strange sight of Crocker shrouded in darkness as they passed through. Cars were parked on the side of the road, and he saw not a soul on the streets. An instant ghost town.

Carol's tongue hit a certain spot, sending shivers through his body and focusing his mind on his wife. She moaned, her voice producing pleasant vibrations as he stroked her hair.

"I wonder if there is a power outage."

His voice was more relaxed now, but Carol paused. "Wow. Still hung up on the lights? Am I that bad?"

Travis laughed. "No, by all means, please continue."

He turned on the radio; Simon & Garfunkel's "Kodachrome" was playing. Soon he had passed the town high school and from there the city limits sign. He took a moment to close his eyes once they had made it through the strangely dark and lifeless place. His focus drifted to his wife's wonderful oral skills.

About seven minutes later he was building, and he knew he could not hold it much longer. The truck's engine began to sputter and knock. The headlights flickered.

"Fuck!" he exclaimed, dropping the transmission into neutral. His lights illuminated a mailbox and driveway on the right, and he'd coasted into it. The truck sputtered to a stop parallel to a detached garage.

Carol had lifted her head from her husband's lap and looked around. "What's going on?"

She reached for her glasses and scanned the dark and silent property. To their right was a barn in the early stages of dilapidation, having endured time and the elements.

"Where are we?"

"In front of someone's house. I don't know where, but the truck stalled." He was nervous as he put himself back together.

"Wait here. I'm going to knock on the door and ask for help."

"Are you sure?"

"Yes, I'm sure."

He opened the door and stepped onto the gravel driveway. His head was on a swivel. They were in a valley. To his right, the land sloped up and he noticed the moon poking through the thick foliage. He opened the gate to the welded wire fence and continued his advance to the front door of the house. He noticed everything, especially how still it was. How silent. There wasn't even a faint breeze or the sound of leaves rustling.

His heart pounded as he knocked on the door. Laquey and Crocker were towns cut from the same cloth. The occupants would be inclined to help a stranger in need, but just as inclined to suspect a person knocking on their door at—he realized he did not know the time. He looked at his watch with the aid of moonlight, just barely making out the hands of his watch. It was 10:32 p.m. He knocked again. No answer. He waited a few moments more before knocking a third time.

He shook his head. They were either too fast asleep or arming themselves against an intruder. He turned his back on the door and headed back to his truck and wife. He scanned the hill and thought the moon was even larger than before. He lost sight of it for a moment, and then he heard his truck come back to life. He then forgot all about the moon.

Travis could see the red light from the taillights glowing around the corner of the garage. Heading straight to the driver's side door, he opened it and slid inside.

"That was strange," he said as he shut the door.

"Yes, let's get out of here," Carol replied, anxiety creeping into her tone.

He put the truck in reverse, backed onto the road, put it in drive, and pressed on to the resort.

* * *

About 50 minutes later, the newlyweds pulled up to the lobby door. They were surprised that the bar was closed and no one was milling about. The couple waited as another set of newlyweds checked in.

"And again, congratulations on your wedding Mr. and Mrs. Bierman," the clerk said as she handed over the key to one of the bridal suites.

"Thank you, we will," Mr. Bierman said, taking his wife by the hand as they headed to the bridal suites. He had shed his tuxedo jacket and rolled up his sleeves.

Travis saw the man's anchor tattoo, and he nodded to the squid.

"Next!" the clerk called and beckoned to the Deacons.

"Your clock is off," Travis said, reaching for his wallet.

"It is?" she responded, confused. She looked at her watch. "I've got 3:02 a.m. What time do you have?"

"It's 11—" His voice trailed as he looked at his watch, realizing the clerk was right.

May 25, 1977

It had been a long road getting to the maternity room of St. John's Hospital in Lebanon, Missouri, even if it was only 30 minutes away from their home in Laquey. It had taken years for Carol to get pregnant—long enough that she had completed her degree and certification as a nurse. It was all worth it when Travis laid their daughter in her hands. A skull cap covered the newborn's wisps of coppery red hair.

"I love you," Travis said as he kissed his wife's forehead and she snuggled their newborn baby.

Chapter One

Mary Deacon was a precocious child. She started walking and talking around nine months. When she was three, her parents took her to a drive-in to watch *The Empire Strikes Back*. Travis and Carol thought their little girl would fall asleep, but instead the three-year-old engaged with the movie and was totally enthralled by the story on the giant screen. From that point on, she was obsessed with the franchise and space in general.

"So, what do you want for Christmas?" Carol asked her daughter one cold winter's day as she did the dishes.

The child thought for a moment. "Another tauntaun."

"Why another one?"

"Well, I has one for Luke. Now Han needs one."

She looked at her daughter, admiring how her kindness extended to her plastic figures. "Are you looking forward to *Revenge of the Jedi*?"

"Uh-huh!" she said excitedly, thinking about the new movie coming out. "Mommy, someday I want to go back to the stars."

Her mother fixed her with a strange look. "Mary, you've never been to outer space. Only astronauts go to space."

"Then I wanna be astronaut."

Her mother smiled. "No, you have to be an adult to become an astronaut."

Mary listened, but she was not buying her mother's story. "But we already go to space. Me and you."

Carol softly laughed at her daughter's creative streak. "Oh? Was Daddy there too?"

It was Mary's turn to laugh. "Oh, Mommy, no. It was just you, the funny people, and me."

"Oh? And what did we do with the funny people?"

"Well, they said they had to open you up, but I could look at the stars."

Carol froze and looked at her five-year-old. The story was, of course, crazy. But it matched a nightmare from two nights earlier.

"What did these funny people look like?"

"They had these big heads. Black eyes. Bigger than me, but not big as you. And very skinny."

Carol's hands, submerged under the bubbles of the dishwater, began to tremble.

* * *

The nightmare had begun with light. It was a bright bluish light that filled the room.

"Shit, not again!" she said as she started to shake Travis, trying to wake him up.

But he was too deeply asleep. She heard the scurrying sound of something in her bedroom. The warmth of the tears sliding down her face was so vivid that she had to question if this was one of the recurring nightmares she had had since she was a little girl.

She looked at her husband's dresser, catty-cornered between the bedroom door and the closet.

"What is it about *me?*" she asked the empty space.

Instead of silence, her question was answered by the sound of movement. Four pale, gray fingers appeared on the back, left corner of the dresser and slowly began to move. A creature revealed itself.

Two soulless, black voids were where its eyes should be. They peered at her. Two small slits ran perpendicular to another resembling a mouth. She stared at it, trying to decipher if it was wearing clothing or not. If it wore clothes, the fabric blended perfectly with the color of its skin. It moved toward the bed she shared with her husband with grace, almost as if gliding through the air. It touched her head, and a calm washed over her body. And, as if on command, she lay down.

She felt weightless as she started to hover above her bed. When she started to move, the door opened to reveal another one of the gray-skinned beings standing there. She heard a giggle.

"We going on a trip, Mommy!"

It was Mary, holding the hand of the strange being. Carol tried to scream, but her mouth would not open, and her vocal cords refused to work. Travis did not move while she quietly sobbed as she was pushed downstairs and out the front door. Hovering about 15 feet above the ground was an otherworldly craft, not making a sound.

The remainder of the nightmare came in snippets. A gleaming hall. Doors that slid open without a sound. The sterile smell. A room that felt, if not looked, like an operating theater. The sensation of not being able to move. More gray-skinned creatures. A voice in her head telling her that everything was all right. That her daughter was safe. That she was safe. More tears streaming down her cheeks. A machine hanging in mid-air, its medicinal-looking instruments swirling about a ball-shaped center.

Then she was in her own bed, fully awake and in control of her body. The warmth of her husband was beside her, the sound of his soft snoring filling the silence. He moved. She got out of bed, her legs shaky and unsure.

Carol went to the master bathroom and refreshed herself, shaking off the rapidly fading memories of the nightmare. On her way back to bed she stopped by her daughter's room. Mary was deep in sleep, a smile on her face.

"It was just a nightmare," she said out loud, trying to convince herself.

* * *

"The funny men said I was healthy and Mommy was healthy."

Mary's words brought Carol back to the present.

"But did not say anything about Daddy."

Carol looked at her daughter in disbelief as fear gripped her heart.

"Mommy, what wrong?"

Chapter Two

Mary's heart pounded as she ran on the dirt road that led to her parent's house. They had moved into the house when she was seven and in the second grade. She knew it had always been her parent's dream to own acreage and raise cattle. Now they owned 100 acres and raised 20 beef cows. Her father had overseen the construction of a large ranch-style house.

Situated in the foothills of the Ozark Mountains, Mary used the gravel road to run and develop herself as a competitor in the sport. She looked forward to the next three years of her high school cross-country career. Laquey was a small school, so even freshmen could make the varsity teams. Her rookie year ended with disappointment when she missed going to the state competition by two seconds at the conference meet.

She swore that she would not miss going her sophomore year. These hills were her secret weapon; they were tough as hell on her muscles, but they made her fast. No one touched her on the flat track, but she yearned for distance running. Her goal was to run a half marathon before the end of the summer. Once school started, running for her high school team meant she could not run in non-school-sanctioned races.

Mary was running faster than usual. It *felt* different. Like she was being stalked. The sensation started about a quarter mile into her run, once she was out of sight of her home and her father tending to some of the cattle in the field.

The hair on the back of her neck bristled, standing on end as she pushed herself up the hills. Intermittently she could hear something in the woods, as if it were keeping up with her.

It's all in your head, Mary. Nothing is in these woods. You have run them hundreds of times before. You have walked them with Daddy. Her internal monologue was only a futile attempt at calming her nerves.

She reached the turnaround point at two-point-five miles, and in a wide arc she turned and started running toward home. As she did, she thought she caught sight of something out of the corner of her eye, reflecting sunlight through the leaves as it ran through the woods. She turned her head to look and saw nothing.

See, nothing! Just your imagination. She silently reassured herself again. *Still, it may not be all that bad to pick up the pace a little.*

Mary pushed herself up and down the steep hills as her breathing became irregular. She was sweating. Her red ponytail swished against the back of her neck. She kept hearing something in the woods; it almost sounded like a wolf. That made her feel somewhat better. There were many feral dogs in the area, and if one was running with her and had not attacked her, it was probably in a playful mood.

Mary crested the final hill, and in a quarter mile she would be home. She saw her father on his tractor. She smiled, feeling safe, as she ran between two hayfields of grass just higher than her knees. She could slow down and still post one of her best practice times, but she was a competitor. When the finish line was in sight, she sped up, not slowed down. She kept her focus on the post her father had painted white to mark both her starting and finishing line. She would not even turn her head, even though she heard the dog that she was convinced was running with her in the grass to her right.

Coach had drilled this focus into his runners. Turning her head slowed her down. It gave away that she did not feel confident in her lead. This had been what cost her two seconds at conference. Mary had turned her head, hearing another runner catching up with her. She slowed. The other girl, smiling, poured on the speed and blasted past her into the finishing gate and went to state. Mary did not.

She had not slowed until she was 20 yards beyond the fence post. Coming to a stop, she caught her breath and then kept walking, feeling proud of her time.

"See? Not bad, eh, fella?" she asked as she breathed heavily, turning to look at the stray that had followed her.

Nothing was there. She shielded her eyes from the glare of the sun as she scanned the windblown grass. She almost missed it at first. The gray face of a wolf blending into the light and shadow of the grass. She locked eyes with it, and they stared at each other.

"Mary!"

She turned her head to yell back. "I'll be right there, Daddy!"

She did not want to completely take her eyes from where the wolf sat, concealed by the tall grass. But she lost contact for the briefest second, and the wolf was gone.

July 15, 1992

It was dark. Too dark. Mary awoke, looking up at the ceiling. Usually, the glossy white paint reflected at least some moonlight. She looked to the left, then the right. Her alarm clock read 3:01 a.m. in bright red digital numbers. Her gaze returned to the ceiling. She felt movement on her bed. She looked down and saw a creature, on all fours, crawling toward her.

She—somehow Mary sensed the creature was female—stopped as Mary caught her creeping closer.

She was gray with a willowy body and long, slender limbs. Supported on a lithe neck was an oversized head—a bulbous and ridiculous head. She stared at Mary with unblinking black eyes that seemed to absorb all light like miniature black holes. The face was featureless. A two to three inch slit formed the mouth, and two much smaller slits parallel to each other but perpendicular to the mouth approximated a nose.

Mary's eyes suddenly rolled back into her head as she passed out.

* * *

Mary awoke again, this time floating through the air, light as a feather. But when she tried to move, she was as stiff as a board. She could only move her eyes as she slowly became aware of her surroundings. She was still in her bedroom, which was flooded with intensely bright light. It was like looking at an x-ray of her house.

Then she saw more figures moving *through* the walls. The creature stepped into view as she hovered in midair. The creature looked just over five feet tall, but the newcomers were shorter and darker in color. They surrounded her, and then she began to move through her home.

Her house was one and a half stories, with the upstairs consisting of three rooms that felt more like an apartment than an integral part of the house. This gave the 15-year-old a sense of independence and privacy, but at that moment it felt like a liability. She tried to scream for her parents but could not move her lips. She felt a tear slide down one side of her face, then another.

She was levitated down the stairs, and she could hear her mother's screams. She caught a glimpse of her parents as she passed their room. Her father was sound asleep. Once more she tried to scream but found herself too paralyzed. Her mother looked like she had more freedom of movement, but not much. She was surrounded by six of the smaller creatures and one taller one that Mary sensed was male. He was hunched over the older woman and appeared to be operating on her, but without having cut her open.

Carol could move little, but she could scream. She screamed with a piercing mix of fear and pain that was too much for whatever force was holding them to completely immobilize her.

How can Daddy be sleeping through this? Mary thought as he remained motionless through the horror happening in his own bed.

She saw the front door open and was pushed outside and into an intense bright light. She felt herself rising.

* * *

Mary awoke for the third time. The sun was shining through her window, and she could hear birds. She looked at her alarm clock, now reading 8:32 a.m. She stretched, suddenly remembering her nightmare. She brushed it off.

She slid out of bed wearing the shorts and t-shirt she had slept in. She stretched and went downstairs to brush her teeth. She tried to not think about how fast the summer was going by. In a month it would be late August, and a new school year would begin.

"—telling you, I heard nothing. I felt nothing. If you were screaming, I would have woken and kicked their ass!"

Mary heard her father.

Travis was angry but trying to keep his voice down.

"But Travis, it was *so* real!" her mother pleaded. "Perhaps Mary heard something?"

She heard her father's hand slam down on the countertop. "Damn it, Carol! You will *not* bring her into this!"

"Bring me into what?" Mary asked, suddenly making her presence known.

Her parents stopped arguing. Her father threw his hands up in disbelief and defeat before turning his back to finish frying some bacon.

"Did you hear me screaming last night? Did you see anything," Carol hesitated, "out of the ordinary?"

Mary felt herself become lightheaded. She braced herself against the wall. How could she have shared a dream with her mother? Yes, everything about it felt like it was happening instead of a dream, but it was too fantastic to be real. It would be a bad idea to share what she knew—she could sense that. But here were her parents fighting about it, and her mother claiming to have experienced the same exact thing. It felt like something in Mary's subconscious was trying to break free into her waking memory.

"I woke up last night to," Mary choked on her words, "strange beings. One was—" Mary stopped again. "H-h-his hands were inside you! You were screaming! You could move a little, and I tried to move but I couldn't, and I saw Daddy and he wouldn't wake up!"

Her father stopped cooking and had turned to see all color drained from the faces of his wife and daughter. "And what exactly were you doing during all of this?" he asked, his tone irritated and perhaps a hair more accusatory than he intended.

"They had me!" Mary cried, defensive. "I floated by as they took me outside! Then there was a bright light, and th-then I woke up."

A tear slid down her cheek, knowing she was telling the truth but knowing he would not believe her.

Chapter Three

November 5, 1992

Mary slipped into the passenger seat of her mom's 1990 Ford Taurus after the class 2 state cross-country championship meet ended. She leaned back in the cloth bucket seat and took a deep breath, still sweating a little.

"I'm proud of you, kiddo," Carol said as she slipped the key in the ignition and started the car, cranking the heat. It was 30°, and while Mary was still sweating from the race, this would soon surrender to the freezing temperature.

"Thanks, Mom." Her tone was a little dejected.

"Sweetie, you're a sophomore. You did amazing. Those other girls were seniors." Reaching over, Carol brushed some errant hair from her daughter's eyes. "If you keep up your level of training, you'll be winning first place by your junior year."

Mary looked out the window.

"Speaking of training, I've noticed you've been running at school and in town instead of down our road. Anything wrong? Did something happen?"

"No." Mary hesitated. "Yes." A deep sigh. "Maybe so. I don't know."

"That's cryptic, even for a moody teen," Carol said with a smile. She put the car in reverse and backed out so they could beat the buses. "You can tell me." She braced herself for what could have caused her very competitive daughter to suddenly stop challenging herself on their country road.

"You're going to think I'm crazy."

Carol shook her head and took a deep breath. "Does it have to do with our shared nightmare from over the summer?"

"No. But just before that, I was on a run and thought something was following me—stalking me."

Mary's words made Carol grip the steering wheel tight enough her knuckles turned white.

"I kept hearing something in the woods and seeing it out of the corner of my eye. It totally weirded me out." Sporting a melancholy expression, she looked out the window.

Carol wanted to pull over but remained calm, trying not to freak out her daughter.

"I thought it was a dog, but when I got to the finish post I saw a wolf. It locked eyes with me and just stared at me. The strangest thing was just how black her eyes were. How *much* of her eyes was black." She shivered.

Carol was quiet, collecting her thoughts. "Mary," her voice started slow and measured, "is this the first time you have seen a wolf?"

Mary looked down, inspecting her fingernails as she sorted through her own thoughts. "No and yes." She looked up and out the window. "No, because I have seen this wolf before. I know because of the pattern of white, gray, and black on her face. Yes, because it was the first time I'd seen her during the day."

"All the other times were at night? Were you sleeping?"

"Yes."

A tear slid down Carol's cheek. "Looking through your bedroom window?"

Mary shot her mother with an incredulous expression. "How? How do you know?"

It was time for Carol to sigh like a moody, melancholy teenager. "My animal was this owl. Growing up, this damn thing started showing up at night. Staring in my window. Then I saw it during the day. When I saw it, I *knew* it was going to happen again and soon."

"What, Mom? What was going to happen?"

The older woman's anxiety proved infectious as Mary became clearly agitated.

"They will pay you—I mean us—a visit."

"Who are they, Mom? What do they want with us?" Mary practically whimpered.

Carol could not think of a ready answer. "Honestly? I do not know. I'm sorry, dear. I wish I did, but I don't."

"What does Daddy think of all this?"

Carol scoffed. "He doesn't. He doesn't believe. He thinks that it's all in my head." She shook her head, mimicking her husband's dismissiveness. "I don't blame him. I mean—" she paused, looking for the right words. "I mean the notion that aliens are abducting me and now you is hard to believe."

"Wait, so you think they are aliens? Like from another planet?"

Mary was processing the new information. It seemed incredible but also correct somehow. She would often wonder what her gray tormentors were. Angels, demons, and even goblins had been possibilities she'd let herself consider.

"I think so. I've seen their spaceships."

"Wow." Mary was stunned. "When was the first time you were, uh, taken?"

"When I was a little girl. It started with the owl. Then one night I woke up and one was on my bed."

Mary shook her head. "Like last July."

Carol nodded. "Like last July." She softly continued "I wanted to talk with you about it then—"

"—but Daddy didn't want to hear it," Mary interrupted, finishing her mother's sentence.

"No. Like I said, he doesn't like to talk about it."

"But why is this happening, Mom? I know you don't know for sure, but don't you have some idea?"

Mary recognized her mother's thoughtful stare and remained silent, allowing her the space to think.

"You know," Carol finally spoke, "how you love Shark Week?"

"Yeah?"

"I think it's a lot like that. They come here and tag us to learn about us, kind of like how they tag great whites and release them." Carol paused before becoming more confident in her answer. "Yeah, something like that. And maybe they only care about the women? Or maybe certain families have something in their bloodline that they are tracking?"

"Could they be manipulating us then? Breeding us like we breed cattle?"

Carol smiled at the natural conclusion of a girl raised on a cattle ranch—even one as small as theirs. Genetics was a major concern when Travis would rent a bull to breed his herd. Still, the notion that her daughter thought they were possibly breeding stock for an alien race disturbed her more than her own idea of being targeted by extraterrestrial zoologists.

"I don't know. I want nothing more in the world than to look you in the eye and tell you that no, that's not what's going on. But I just don't know." Carol took a deep breath. "If they are here, I think that they are most likely here for science. I cannot say this for sure, but it is nice to believe."

"But how, Mom? How could they be here? Space is big. Like really, really big."

"Listen, I know I'm not much of an intellectual. I'm just a nurse from Laquey, Missourah." She adopted a playful but sarcastic tone. "But I know the earth is old and the universe is older. If God created the universe 12 billion years ago and the Earth four billion years ago, how advanced would a civilization created like a million or a billion years before us be?"

"I guess that they could make a spaceship that could make that trip." Mary's voice trailed off.

She loved her mother for being the smartest person she knew, but at times the challenge of keeping up could be exhausting. Additionally, the topic made her feel uncomfortable if not violated.

"Could we talk about something else?"

Carol could tell she went too far, and she felt guilty. "Sure, honey." She saw a Burger King a couple hundred yards away. "What do you say to stopping for a milkshake?"

Her daughter smiled. "That sounds wonderful."

Chapter Four

Mary danced as closely as she could with her date, Jason Farmer, on the blue tarp laid over the wooden floor of the high school gymnasium for the Valentine's Day dance. She danced in bare feet, having shed her heels in favor of comfort. The Europop rhythm of Right Said Fred had the kids on the floor dancing like fools.

The kids clapped as the song ended, and Mary looked up at Jason, their eyes meeting. She felt something. Something different. She had been attracted to him for some time, but in that moment the attraction was undeniable. She smiled, her innocent smile touched by desire for the first time. Softer notes began to play, driving those with dates into each other's arms.

"I love this movie," Mary said, her hands wrapped around his neck.

His hands wrapped around her waist as they swayed to Bryan Adams's love theme to *Robin Hood: Prince of Thieves*.

"Me too. Next time you come over to study, we could take a break and watch it."

Mary blushed. "Well, you asked me to proofread your paper for Ms. Lincoln, and I could use some quizzing for our chemistry final."

Studying had been a convenient excuse to spend time together. Both were too awkward to admit they had feelings for each other. He was good at math and chemistry. She connected well with biology, social studies, and English. So, while they did help one another, the fact that they were able to do things like watch movies while sitting close to each other was a pleasant side effect.

The only problem was his father: Master Sergeant Thomas Farmer, assigned to the Combat Engineers Advanced Individual Training School at Fort Leonard Wood. The family had been assigned there since shortly before Jason's freshman year, which meant they were likely to be reassigned soon.

They danced in silence, just enjoying being close to each other. As Bryan Adams finished his ballad, Jason took her by the hand and led her to the gym door.

"Where are we going?" she asked, as the catchy, repetitive chords of "Two Princes" by the Spin Doctors began to play.

Jason said nothing as Mary let him lead her away from the crowded dance floor. Her heart thundered in her chest, and she wanted to question what they were doing but the words would not come. She saw he was leading her to the parking lot, and she too suddenly felt the need to get somewhere private.

"Hold on, let me get my shoes."

He released her hand, and she practically skipped to get her heels. When she came back, she fumbled awkwardly while putting them on before taking his hand.

Before either of them knew it, they were at his truck.

"So, what n—" She had not finished her sentence before he spun her around and wrapped his arms around her, pulling her close and pressing his lips against hers.

It was the passionate first kiss she had wanted from him for so long. She wrapped her arms around his neck and kissed him back. Her eyes closed, foot theatrically lifting off the ground. It seemed to go on forever.

Jason pulled away, his nervousness returning. He hoped that he had not crossed a line. He was relieved to see her smiling.

"So, do you want to go back inside? There's still an hour left."

"Or," she took his hand and led him around to the passenger side door, "you could take me home and," she paused to look up at him, "get lost on the way?"

He looked at her with only brief confusion before grinning. "Yes, ma'am," he answered in the cheesy tone of a teenage boy trying to sound cool for the girl he loves.

* * *

Mary's father rented 50 acres from an old man who had retired from ranching but did not want to give up his ancestral land. About a mile from home, the road split. To the right was home and the end of a perfect night. To the left was the gate to the pasture where her father used to grow hay. The gate was 50 yards from the road and concealed by trees. Jason turned the truck off, and she slid over into his lap. She had her arms wrapped around his neck, allowing his hands to explore her body freely.

Neither one was sure of how far they would go, but both were afraid and excited by how far they *wanted* to go.

His hands moved up her side, seeking out her breast with his left hand. His right hand was bolder; starting with her knee, he slowly slid up her nylon clad leg. She parted them, encouraging further exploration.

Suddenly her head jerked back, hitting the glass of the driver side window. Unwanted memories began to flood her mind. Memories of her on her back on a gurney. Five of the gray beings looking down at her. A strange ball hovering above her. Mechanical arms with strange instruments swirling above her. Her legs held apart as four slender fingers reached for one of the ball's appendages, one that ended with a light.

She pressed her knees together, catching Jason's hands between her thighs. He looked at her, filled with terror that he had done something wrong.

"No! Let me go! Don't touch me!"

She began thrashing in her date's arms. He pulled his hand from the vice-like grip of her upper thighs and held his hands up.

As she squirmed, her gaze fell to a seemingly terrified and confused Jason. "Oh, Jason, I'm so sorry. That-that wasn't you. It was a bad memory."

"Wha-what happened?" His voice trembled.

"Something," she faltered, "something bad happened to me. I-I—" she stammered, not knowing what to say.

He wrapped his arms around her. "It's okay, you're safe. I'm not going to do anything you don't want to." He pulled her close, his hands no longer exploring her body but holding her protectively. "I'm not going to let anything happen to you. I'll protect you."

She buried her face in his chest, thinking to herself: *If only you, or someone, could.*

Chapter Five

In a rare act of sneaky defiance, Mary had stolen a copy of the gate key to the field they had parked in a month earlier. They had seen a movie, *Fire in the Sky*, about the Travis Walton alien abduction story. After a dinner at the Ryan's Steakhouse outside of the fort, they had retreated to the field. Jason put the truck in park and before he could say anything, she had slid into his lap and wrapped her arms around him as she pressed her lips to his.

After five minutes, his hands freely roaming above her waist, he pulled away. "So," he said in a confident, playful voice, the awkwardness having fallen away weeks ago after their third and fourth dates, "I thought it was funny how Mr. Walton's name is Travis." He laughed.

Mary looked away, a pained look on her face.

He reached for her chin and pulled her face toward him, making eye contact. "What is going on with you? I can tell something is wrong." His green eyes bore into her brown ones. "You can tell me anything." He moved his hand away from her chest to hold her more tenderly. "I want to be here for you, if you'll just let me in."

"What makes you think anything is wrong?"

"I still think about the last time we were here—the night of the dance. All of a sudden you started, I don't know, fighting me? Like I was trying to," he couldn't bring himself to say the word, "hurt you. And then the mood shifted so suddenly, and I just held you while you cried."

"That was then? What makes you think something is wrong tonight?"

He cocked his head to one side in disbelief. "For one, I saw the same look on your face just minutes ago that I did that night. And while we're at it, ever since we left the movie and turned off Highway 17, you haven't stopped scanning the fields and the sky."

Her eyes broke the lock which held them.

He chuckled. "Are you afraid of being abducted by aliens?"

Her eyes snapped back to his, and a shudder ran through her body.

His expression turned puzzled. "Wait, *are* you?"

She looked away in silent answer.

"You are." His voice was quiet. "Should we not have gone to the movie?"

"You wouldn't believe me," she finally said. "I knew going to see that movie was a mistake. But I can't explain it. I *needed* to see it."

"Why?"

She took a deep breath. "I've seen," she hesitated, "things. I've woken up in the middle of the night and seen *them* in my room."

"*Seriously?*" he asked, his tone incredulous. He leaned back in his seat.

"I knew I shouldn't have told you." She started to move off his lap. "I knew you wouldn't believe me."

He wrapped his arms tighter around her, trying to pull her closer to him. "Look, it's not that I don't believe you. It's just, I mean, this is crazy." He shook his head immediately as if he knew he'd just made a mistake. "Not that *you're* crazy, but the situation is crazy."

"Good save," she said, stifling a sniffle.

"This," he glanced out the window, "this is just *a lot*. So, do you remember anything else? Were they just watching you? What were they doing?"

She looked away, unable to bring herself to look at him.

"I was taken. Mom said we've been—"

"Wait, your *mother* has been taken too?"

Solemnly she nodded. "Yes. She says she has been taken several times. Since she was a little girl. Like me."

"What—" he had to dig deep to marshal the nerve to finish the question, afraid knowing the answer would horrify him, "what do they do?"

She took a deep breath, gathering her courage to answer. "I think they have done tests—sexual tests. That's why I freaked out after the dance."

Jason took a deep breath before answering. "That makes sense."

"Think more medical and scientific than rape." She whispered the last word.

He said nothing. Instead, he pulled her close and just held her. Finally, he spoke. "It's okay. We'll figure this out."

Chapter Six

After several months of the cold shoulder from one of her best friends, Mary had buried the hatchet with Leanne Sanderson. Best friends since elementary school, they became "frenemies" when both girls began crushing on Jason, and Mary had won the competition—a competition Mary was not aware of until she finally decided to try repairing the relationship.

"So, you've been tired lately around school. Lots of hot nights with Jason?"

Leanne was not quite so forgiving, so she fished for dirt on Mary that would be sexual in nature.

Mary had been emboldened to trust more after her admission to Jason and his understanding.

"Actually, we haven't done much. I mean we have done some." She giggled. "I've given him some, um, blowjobs."

"You *slut*!" Leanne squealed. "But have you done *it* yet?"

"No, I'm a virgin. Sort of."

"Sort of?"

Mary closed her eyes and took a deep breath. "I was abducted."

"Abducted?" A sincere expression of concern spread across Leanne's face, thinking Mary had been abducted by a local—assuming she was talking about a *human* abductor.

"Yes, they came down and took me. There was a part-human alien who," Mary avoided eye contact, "did stuff to me."

Leanne smirked as she now only pretended to listen with concern. She had considered turning off the tape recorder she had hidden behind her back, but this was too good to be true. No way someone this *crazy* could attract someone like Jason and keep him interested. She had struck gold.

May 3, 1993

Mary came into school looking forward to seeing Jason. He had spent the weekend on a father-son trip with his dad, so she had not spoken with him since Thursday. She turned the corner to the hallway lined with lockers, bumping into him.

"Mary! You-you got here early!"

"Yes, I wanted to see you." She looked around and, seeing no teachers or staff, got on her tiptoes and gave him a peck on the lips.

"Um, let's go the other way."

"I need to drop my books off and—" Mary's jaw dropped as she stepped around him and saw her locker.

There were silver and blue streamers on it. Green balloons taped to it.

"What happened?"

One of the balloons twisted, and she saw the black eyes and slits for nose and mouth. A tear came to her eyes.

"It was Leanne! She—"

Before he could spit it out, the PA crackled to life. *"I was abducted."* Leanne had edited her voice off the tape. *"Yes, they came down and took me. There was a part-human alien who did stuff to me."*

Mary looked up at her boyfriend for a moment as tears filled her eyes. She took off in a sprint toward the doors and out to Jason's car.

Chapter Seven

Mary climbed into the deer stand and just watched the cattle graze. The weather was hot, and she broke a sweat walking to her spot. The two-person deer stand was where her father brought her to teach her how to hunt. She was a country girl. She had learned to drive when she was 10. She drove her father's F-150 in the field to haul hay as he and one or two high school boys he hired from their church tossed the square bales onto the flat-bed trailer. She banded male calves, helping with turning them from bulls into steers.

The work needed to get done, so when she was big enough, she was pressed into service doing what she could to help. This gave her a sense of independence, of being able to navigate the woods on her own. That she carried a shotgun gave her a sense of safety against nature and the predators Mother Nature harbored. The deer stand also gave her a safe haven to go to when she wanted to disconnect from the world and just *be*. And be alone. No one around. Just her thoughts.

She was heartbroken. Jason's departure was not sudden. They had known it was coming back in May when his father got orders to Fort Bragg, North Carolina. That had been one of the reasons she had been hesitant in pursuing a relationship with him. She had kissed him goodbye before he got in the car with his father to start the cross-country trip. She got in her little Ranger, left post, and drove straight home.

She was glad her mom was at work and her father was working at the leased field so they did not see her crying as she entered the house. She traded her sundress for jeans and a t-shirt and began packing a backpack for her hike to the tree stand. She took the slipcover off her recently acquired copy of *Star Wars: The Last Command* and put that in her bag along with a peanut butter and jelly sandwich. Finally, she grabbed her 12 gauge and took off for the tree stand.

The first thing she did was allow herself a good cry. A full sob. She had grown close to Jason. It was the first time she had felt like she had truly fallen in love, and he told her the same thing. She had never become comfortable with the idea of penetration, so they never had sex and he did not push it. However, they had found other ways to explore and enjoy each other's budding sexuality.

He did express some skepticism about her abductions, eventually offering alternatives like she was repressing some trauma. She had been shocked and asked him why he would think about things like that. His response warmed her heart—he researched the topic.

After getting the sobs out of her system, she began to feel better. She wiped the tears from her eyes before eating her sandwich. She watched the cattle grazing as she ate; a calf playing around its mother lightened her mood. Then she thought about her own childhood and how she was in the last years of it. Soon adulthood would forever claim her. Composing herself, she pulled out her book and proceeded to get lost in a galaxy far, far away and the events that happened there a long time ago. *Star Wars* would keep her young. She lost track of time and soon found herself 20 pages from the end of the novel.

So engrossed was she that she did not notice the sun growing low in the sky. Nor did she notice the wolf watching her. The one with the same gray and black pattern on her face. The same all black eyes. Only when she raised her eyes above the page of her book did she see the creature. Slowly, nonchalantly, she placed the book on the bench next to her. She reached for her shotgun. The animal did not move. Mary shouldered her weapon and drew a bead on her target, her heart racing as her finger slipped into the trigger guard. The wolf just stared at her. She tried to calm herself, take the shot, and be rid of her tormentor. Her aim was steady, developed through years of practice and experience.

She suddenly withdrew her finger from the trigger and dropped the long gun from her shoulder.

"What's the point? If you are what I think you are, you probably have some sort of bulletproof armor. And friends nearby."

She thought she sounded crazy, speaking to a woodland creature she was not even sure existed.

"Whatever. You're just the perfect end to the perfect day," she said in frustration.

Mary put the book and the baggie that carried her sandwich into her backpack and secured the pack in place. She stood, keeping an eye on the wolf. It still had not moved. She climbed down, turning her back to the field the animal was sitting in. She unslung her shotgun and turned around to see if the wolf was still there.

It wasn't.

Chapter Eight

It had been one year since she had awakened to the horror of that creature on her mattress. Besides her mother, Jason had been the only person she felt safe speaking to about the incident. She was still feeling the loss of her confidant. Her father did not want to entertain the possibility that things he did not believe existed had tortured his wife and took his daughter from his house. And he had slept through the ordeal. That was, he had said several times, ludicrous.

She did all she could do to move on with her life while juggling a college prep course load, training to dominate her junior cross-country season, and dealing with strange dreams and the ever-present wolf. The animal never threatened her, just kept pace with her.

Travis bought her a can of mace, and Mary had started running the hilly road again.

Each morning before the heat could climb from unbearable to insufferable, she would put on her favorite pair of running shoes. With her ponytail softly swishing against the back of her neck, she would run on the dirt roads near her house. Mondays, Wednesdays, and Saturdays were her short days. She would only run three miles. Tuesday was a five-mile day, and Friday was her long day, running seven miles. This was the plan given to her by her Coach Kempker.

Each day she would make sure she attempted a particularly difficult hill she had dubbed "Mount Doom." It was about a half a mile long, starting as a gentle slope that got progressively steeper. About three-quarters of the way up, the road took an almost 90-degree turn. This is what made the hill so difficult; it gave the illusion that one was almost done and it was about to become a downhill grade. But then one would get to it and realize that the road merely curved and continued its heartbreaking ascent. Even though she knew this, Mount Doom (being at the end of her three-mile run but not even halfway for her seven-mile run) had tricked her every time she tackled it.

She had yet to conquer Mount Doom, and she was determined today would be the day. She felt refreshed after her rest day. Mary pushed herself, reminded herself that it was only an illusion and that when she made the turn there would be more hill to beat. And she could do it. She closed her eyes as she got nearer to the curve. Maybe if she could not see it, it would not defeat her.

The sound of a soft rustling in the leaves ahead of her was enough to rouse her from her meditation. She opened her eyes; sometimes the neighbor's dog would harass her at this point in her run. Mary was ready to repel it with the can of mace. She saw nothing. Everything was still, and all she could hear was the crunching of gravel beneath her feet. She took a deep breath and willed herself to keep running.

She felt the air filling her lungs with each deep inhalation. She explosively exhaled and pumped her arms, trying to will more speed from her tired body. She glanced behind her to see if the wolf was following her or if she was imagining things. So certain it was the wolf, Mary had just committed Coach Kempker's mortal sin of running: looking behind her.

"First, you can trip because you are not looking where you are going," he would say. "Secondly, and worst of all, it causes you to slow down. You don't win races by slowing down."

As if her coach was a prophet, she stumbled and began falling forward. "Shit!" she yelled as she braced herself against the impact of hitting the ground.

The impact never came.

She was floating face down about six inches from the gravel road. Then she was rising. When it seemed like she was hovering about two feet from the road, she slowly began to turn. Then she saw them. The same gray, skinny creature from that horrible night a year earlier and six of her kind slowly emerged from the woods.

Next came the humming, as if from another world. The beings escorted her off the road toward the woodline. Toward the hum. She was completely immobilized again; all she could move were her eyes. As they cleared the other side of the woodline, she saw the source of the humming: a slate gray cylindrical-shaped craft hovering six feet from the earth.

A ramp extended from the craft, and she was pushed up it and into the belly of the craft. She was left alone in an all white room furnished only with a small bed onto which she was gently lowered. Her escorts left, and only after the door closed was she able to move. She ran to where the door had been. She could not even see its seams. It was like the wall just opened and then closed back in on itself.

Defeated, she walked back over to the bed and curled into the fetal position. She began to cry. Moments later the wall opened back up and a tall *man* entered. He was a perfect human specimen save for a bluish tint to his skin. He wore a black, skintight uniform and looked at her, smiling as he crossed the room.

Mary backed up against the wall, more terrified by his presence than the grays. Her terror did not deter him. As he got close enough, he reached for her and gently caressed her cheek.

* * *

Mary awoke being lifted from the road to see blood on the ground. She thought at first it was the same invisible force that had held her immobilized. But then her arm twitched freely, and she realized that she was being held by familiar arms.

"Daddy?" she asked.

"Yes, baby-bear," Travis said softly as he carried her to his truck to drive her to the hospital.

The doctor was a little suspicious. He said the cut above her right eye was too straight to have been caused by falling on a rock. He had noticed a spot on her shorts and called in a female doctor to do a physical. They had told Mary that it was just a routine check to see if she had any other injuries covered up by her clothing. The female doctor was delicate and gentle as she examined her.

"Did you see anyone?" she asked softly.

"No, ma'am," Mary responded softly, unable to look the woman in the eyes. She would not dare to tell the truth.

"When was the last time you had sex?" the doctor asked in a manner too nonchalant for Mary's liking.

"I'm a virgin," Mary responded.

The doctor placed a hand on Mary's and gave it a soft squeeze. She finished the physical and left Mary to get dressed again while she informed Mary's parents that their daughter had been raped.

* * *

Looking down at the pregnancy test and seeing the plus sign was not what upset her. Having to drop out of cross-country when she was favored to set new records that year was not the worst part of what had happened to her. The worst part was not having anyone to talk to about it. Even her mother had difficulty discussing it. The town knew. There were whispers. Some of the boys preened and boasted about how they would beat the guy who did it to a pulp. Some of the girls gossiped that Mary was just covering for a secret boyfriend she was sleeping with.

She no longer rode the bus. She continued to run, but her father followed her in his truck with a shotgun by his side. She tried to run with the cross-country team, but the school would not accept the liability, so she ran on her own. It helped her deal with what had happened. She even finally conquered Mount Doom. It was a Tuesday. She had even set a personal record.

Her father walked her into the house where her mother was taking a nap on the couch.

"I'm going to run and get pizza," he said in a whisper. "Your mom's here, so you'll be safe."

"Okay, Daddy."

She went to hug him—a game they played when one of them was disgustingly dirty, like after a day of hauling hay or conquering Mount Doom. He backed out the door, sharing in the innocent fun, shutting the door behind him. As the doorknob clicked, she turned and started for the stairs. Five seconds later she was almost to the bathroom when she heard a key in the lock.

She turned and as the door opened, she began to ask, "What did you forg—" The words got stuck in her throat.

Her father was carrying two pizzas. And she suddenly felt rather empty.

Chapter Nine

Mary's body fought sleep. She was too excited. The next day Mary and her parents would board a plane for Indiana and orientation at Notre Dame. She was going to start her freshman year of college at the private Catholic university on an athletic scholarship for cross-country. Desiring to become a writer, she had enrolled in the College of Arts & Sciences to get a literature degree.

Another advantage was the fact that she was moving far away from the farm. While this was painful, for there were many great memories at her childhood home, she prayed she'd be far away from the aliens. She hoped that she would be free from their random abductions and experiments. While the bad times were outnumbered by the happy times, not having to worry about them was worth leaving her childhood behind. So, when she did get to sleep, it was worry-free.

* * *

Normally a side sleeper, Mary awoke face down. She tried to roll over to greet the day, but she could not move. Slowly she became aware of the sensation of hands holding her down. She felt a prick in the back of her right knee that did not stop at the skin. Mary tried to scream as her body was penetrated by something akin to a wide gauge needle. The pain was searing and intense but only lasted for a moment. Then the hands were gone. Moments later she was able to move on her own. She reached down and rubbed the back of her knee where she had felt the pain. There was a welt, warm and tender to the touch.

Part Two | The Romance of Mary Deacon

Chapter Ten

August 23, 1995

Mary was finding out that the first week of class at college was a lot like the first day of kindergarten. You only knew a few people, and you did not know who to sit next to. She walked into a literature course on speculative fiction. Scanning the classroom, there were a few seats available. One was next to a handsome, athletic-looking guy who appeared eager at the prospect she might sit next to him. Another was a pretty blonde with the judgmental confidence of the popular girl in high school who reminded her of Leanne.

Then there was "the nerd." He sat in the center of the front row, oblivious to all going on around him. He was scribbling in a notebook. He seemed like the perfect choice, plus she found the jock's crestfallen expression at not being picked amusing. She had dressed to turn heads as she redefined herself in a new school in a new state. She wore a dark floral dress, black leggings, black boots, and a choker.

She did indeed turn several heads, much to the seeming irritation of

Leanne 2.0. What shocked her was her chosen neighbor. He did not so much as bat an eye in her direction. She crossed her legs under the desk and adjusted herself as if to get comfortable, hoping that the movement and soft noise would attract his attention. Nothing. She dropped her pencil and leaned over to pick it up. As she slowly sat back in her seat, she caught him looking. She smiled at him. He blushed and returned to his writing. She thought of saying something, but the professor entered.

* * *

Thirty minutes later, with the syllabi handed out and several questions answered, the professor released the class early. She had admonished them that this would not be the norm. Mary's neighbor took his books and started for the door, but Mary followed after. He turned and looked at her. She smiled.

"Hi," he said, his voice quiet but betraying a hidden strength.

"Hello. I'm Mary."

"Di—" he started. "I mean Richard. Richard Fisher."

She laughed. "Do you go by Dick?" She smiled warmly.

He blushed a deep red. "Yes." He shifted his weight from foot to foot as if this was the first time a girl had approached and talked to him.

"It's very nice to meet you. I've got Archeology of the Bible next. What do you have?" She was fishing for information, hoping he had the same class as her.

"I actually don't have another class until after lunch. American Government."

"Oh. Will I see you around?"

"Sure?"

"I look forward to it." She turned and walked away, feeling his eyes on her.

* * *

Archeology of the Bible was not yet filled with students when Mary arrived. Thus, she had to take her chances on who would sit next to her. She was thumbing through the textbook, which she was starting to realize she more than likely did not need, when a shadow passed over her desk. She looked up at the guy who sat next to her. He had blond, feathered hair and steel blue eyes, giving him an almost Nordic look. He wore cargo shorts and a Nirvana t-shirt.

"Hey, my name's Ken. What's yours?"

"Mary."

He smiled. "So, what're you in for?" he quipped.

"Excuse me?"

"What's your major?"

"Literature. You?" She found him more fun and engaging than Dick.

"I'm doing accounting. But gotta knock out these prerequisites. Freshman?"

"Is it that obvious?"

"Well, you do have that lost, wandering look."

She blushed and was about to respond when the professor interrupted.

"Good morning, class." An older, plump man entered and trundled to the podium. "I am Dr. Morgan Essex, and we are going to cover mostly early Christian archeology. However, we are also going to be discussing universal religious symbols and artifacts such as the swastika. Can anyone tell me the earliest use of this symbol? Hint: It is far older than Hitler and the Nazis."

Ken raised his hand, and Dr. Essex pointed at the young man. "Please introduce yourself and take your best guess."

The professor's voice betrayed his doubt. Likely a result of decades of students getting the question wrong, Mary imagined.

"My name is Kenneth Buchwald. I believe there was an ivory figure found with one that dated to 12-15,000 years ago in the Ukraine. Carl Sagan wrote that he thought a comet passed so close to the earth that jets of gas coming off it could be seen. Which is why it appears in Europe, India, and as far as North America."

Mary thought Dr. Essex looked impressed.

"Very well said, Mr. Buchwald." The man looked at Ken. "Are you the son of Ryan Buchwald?"

"Yes, sir."

Ken worried he had put his foot in his mouth. His father was an archaeologist. Despite a reputation of producing sound scholarship, he received criticism that his theories often involved celestial involvement. His father had more detractors than benefactors. Some of his colleagues thought he skirted the fine line between genius and crank.

Mary couldn't help but notice Ken's confidence had taken a hit.

The professor smiled. "I knew your father in graduate school." He switched his focus from Ken to the rest of the class. "Young Mr. Buchwald is absolutely correct. This is but a taste of the ancient mysteries we will delve into in this seminar. Now, let's begin by analyzing how old the earth is both theologically and scientifically."

* * *

Forty-five minutes later, Professor Essex dismissed the class early. He also admonished them not to get used to the extra five minutes.

"You did not tell me you were the son of a preeminent archaeologist," Mary said as she gathered her books and stood up.

"Should I have led with that?"

"No, not at all," she said, accompanied by a soft laugh.

"Mr. Buchwald." Professor Essex's voice boomed as he stepped toward the pair. "Please give my regards to your father. And after this semester you can stop by for dinner with me and Missy." He glanced at Mary. "Perhaps you will bring along this enchanting young lady? Miss?" His voice trailed, and he cocked an eyebrow as if asking a question.

"Mary Deacon." She extended a hand which he shook.

"Miss Deacon." He leaned in conspiratorially to her. "Watch out for this one. If he's like his father, he's a ladies' man. Better reel him in quick if you're interested." Without another word, he once again trundled off, leaving Ken blushing.

"Well, that was awkward." Ken tried to recover.

"Very."

"Would a date be on the table, or did my dad's friend spoil the mood?"

"Mood spoiled? Absolutely. A date? Absolutely."

Ken's expression fell at first before brightening. He smiled again. "Friday night?"

"Sounds lovely. Dinner and a movie I assume?"

"Well, I was thinking something else, not sure what." His voice trailed as he remembered something. "And, uh, perhaps, we can move the date to Saturday?"

"Oh? Was the good professor right in warning me away from you? Do you have another girl on the stringer?" Mary teased.

"No, no, no! I just had, um, other plans that night."

"Sounds mysterious. I'll bite. *The X-Files* doesn't start until next month, so I'm missing my weekly dose of mystery."

"Wait, you watch *The X-Files*?"

"Yeah! And other stuff like *Star Wars* and *Star Trek*. And *Batman*, although I was disappointed in *Batman Returns*. I am nervous about Val Kilmer taking over from Michael Keaton." Mary caught herself rambling.

Ken shook his head in disbelief. "Wow. I did not know they made girls in geek."

Mary feigned offense. "What do you think? That all girls have the same cookie-cutter set of interests?"

"No, I-I'm just not that used to girls being interested in the same stuff I am. That's all. I didn't mean anything by it," Ken quickly explained.

"It's okay. I was born on the day *Star Wars* was released! My mother was—" she caught herself before admitting that she and her mother were alien abductees. "She was always fascinated by the stars. She grew up watching *Star Trek* and reading books about space. Definitely something she passed on to me. So, what are we doing if not dinner and a movie? What mysterious appointment do you have?"

Ken shuffled nervously. "It's an author reading. Winston Franklin is reading from his new book *Fellowship*. It's about—are you okay? Mary, you're pale."

Mary knew all about the investigative journalist Winston Franklin. She had read *The Twelve*, a book about the Majestic-12 conspiracy regarding the government cover-up of the Roswell UFO crash. She had heard about his upcoming book about his own experiences with "the grays."

"Yes, I'm . . . all right. I know who Winston Franklin is. I've been waiting to read his book actually." She locked eyes with him. "Do you believe in aliens? Do you believe they could be abducting humans?"

Ken's expression became pained. "I don't believe they could be." His gaze shifted away from her piercing eyes.

As the lock was broken, she looked away as well, glad that she did not reveal her secret.

"I don't *believe* it. I *know* it."

Her eyes shot back up to his.

"I know it because I have been taken."

Mary's jaw dropped in disbelief. She had never met someone other than her mother who was an "experiencer."

* * *

They left class together, and Ken said he knew of a really great coffee house close to campus. Neither had anywhere to be for hours, so they sat down and leisurely sipped their coffees.

"I still can't believe I met you." He shook his head in disbelief.

Blushing, she looked at her latte. "You make me sound like some sort of unicorn."

"It's just," he looked around before leaning over and speaking in a hushed tone, "I feel like I can tell you that I've seen UFOs and aliens. You know, the gray kind."

Mary remained silent, processing what she was hearing. On one hand, it felt too good to be true to bump into another with similar experiences. On the other hand, she was skeptical and did not want to let her guard down. She had been burned before.

"You don't believe me." Ken slouched back into his seat. "Let me guess, you like the idea but it's just good science fiction for you." His tone was defensive.

"No, it's not that." She looked up and could see that he was bothered by her lack of response. "I want to believe you. It's just incredible that—"

"Incredible?" His tone went up just a little, "Look at how we study animals! Tagging them and releasing them back into the wild. Do you think a shark knows what we're doing?"

A tear slid down her cheek, as she suddenly felt cornered and overwhelmed. "Not what I meant at all! What I find incredible is that I just randomly bumped into another—" she searched for the best word, "experiencer." She took a deep breath and a leap of faith. "My mother and I, we have both been abducted. Several times. Since I was a little girl."

Now it was Ken's jaw that dropped. "Wow. I'm sorry. It's just, you know."

"Yeah."

Nothing else needed to be said. Both just shared an extended silence.

"So, was it the grays that took you and your mom?"

She cast a confused glance his way. "What other kinds of aliens would they be?"

"Have you read much on the subject?"

"No, just Winston's books. He only mentions the grays."

"Well, there are," he swallowed, "others. Some people report seeing reptilian aliens. Much larger, beefier than the slender grays. Others say they see things that are smaller that maybe resemble goblins. There is one story, somewhere out of the South, about a family that claims they were harassed by the goblin creatures for a couple of nights." He took a sip of his coffee. "I thought you were a fan of *The X-Files*? Haven't they had other types of aliens?"

"Yes, but I never took that as . . . real. The same way I don't think Jabba the Hutt is based on a real alien."

"Oh, no? But I bet you would look good in a gold bikini." He winked, causing her to laugh at the much-needed break from the tension.

Chapter Eleven

Mary had spent the day in a flurry of excitement for her date that night. While she could feel Dick's awkward glances in the class they shared, she did not flirt back. She kept glancing up at the clock. For probably the first time ever, Professor Essex's Archaeology of the Bible could not get here soon enough. She did give Dick a quick smile and polite "hello" as their speculative fiction course was released, but she hurried to her next class.

There was an air of muted excitement as Ken met her outside the classroom.

She did not notice Dick following her like a lovelorn puppy. Nor did she see him sulk away to his next course, his shoulders drooped in defeat.

For Ken and Mary, Archeology of the Bible flew by. Ken was emboldened to speak in a successful effort to impress her. He did know a lot about archeology and the ancient world. He would hint at man's fascination with the celestial and the heavens as being based on real phenomena but would stop short of saying it was aliens.

After class, they were both tempted to see if the other was interested in grabbing coffee, but both were too nervous about appearing over eager. So, they went their separate ways until later that evening.

* * *

After her classes were finished, Mary spent the day getting ready for her date. Her roommate was another cross-country runner named Kayla Wagner. The other girl kept the dorm room for appearances since her parents would not approve of premarital cohabitation, but for all intents and purposes, she lived with her boyfriend. This worked out for Mary—it meant she effectively did not have a roommate.

Ken knocked on her door about 10 minutes early, and they left for dinner at Olive Garden before heading to the Holiday Inn where Winston Franklin was delivering his talk. Ken bought his date a hardcover of the book, so she could get it signed along with her battered and dog-eared copy of *The Twelve* at the post-talk signing.

The author stepped onto the raised dais and stood behind the podium with a copy of his book. He was in his mid-40s with salt and pepper hair. He looked distinguished but not in a bookish way. Mary thought he projected the image of a man brought up in the country. When he started speaking, his voice projected power and strength.

"Good evening, ladies and gentlemen. I am Winston Franklin, an investigative journalist turned crackpot."

The room laughed at his self-deprecating humor.

"I started out, just a regular journalist, on the crime beat in Chicago. That then morphed into investigating more … unusual phenomenon. I have had a lifelong fascination with the paranormal and the things that go bump in the night. It started in childhood. I had an Aunt Sara who lived at the end of this dirt road in the deep dark woods of Missouri. We would go and visit every summer. I loved the fresh air.

"This would be the place where I would be abducted for the first time.

I was nine years old. This event takes place in chapter three of *Fellowship*, which is tonight's selected reading." He opened the book to the bookmarked page and began reading. "While it is considered a melodramatic cliché, it really was a dark and stormy night. The rain fell in torrents, except at occasional intervals—"

* * *

Twenty minutes later, Mr. Franklin had finished his chapter and began taking questions. A blond man with a mullet introduced himself as Max and stood.

"Mr. Franklin—"

"Please," he interrupted, "call me Winston."

"Well, Winston, why don't we ever see the grays wearing space suits or clothes of *any* type?"

Winston, along with the rest of the audience, chuckled. "Lots of theories. Perhaps they have outgrown modesty and do not require clothing? Perhaps what we think is skin is actually some sort of spacesuit? For example, we think they have black eyes, but what if those are some sort of eye protection?" He scanned the audience as if looking for another—and better—question.

Mary stood up next, catching the attention of the speaker.

"The beautiful young woman." He smiled.

Mary was too eager to speak to even offer a smile at the compliment. "Mr., I mean, Winston, why? Why are the aliens here? Why abduct humans? Why abduct . . . us?"

"That's a good question." He took the microphone off the podium. "There are many theories. Some think they are here to issue a warning about the destruction of the planet at our hands. Either through pollution, environmental destruction, war, or nuclear apocalypse." He paced across the dais as he continued.

"Others think that they are here to study us like we do primates. They could be extradimensional beings or even future humans who have evolved to be something nearly unrecognizable. They could be belligerents studying us prior to invasion or extorting our governments for natural resources they cannot provide for themselves."

"But which one do *you* think is right?" Max interposed from his seat.

"I guess that they are studying us and guiding our evolution. Perhaps even helping us select the perfect mate."

* * *

A few hours later they were at Ken's apartment, talking about the evening. Mary was excited to have had her books autographed. She leaned against Ken, her head resting on his shoulder. She looked up, their eyes meeting. She smiled in invitation, and he leaned down and kissed her on the lips.

A few minutes later, he broke the kiss. "That was . . . nice." His voice trailed.

"Did it feel weird to you?"

He nodded emphatically in agreement. "Don't take this the wrong way. I mean I'm an only child, so I really don't have a frame of reference—"

"But it felt like kissing your brother? Or in your case sister?" Mary finished, unable to look him in the eye.

"I'm sorry." Ken gave her a squeeze. "It's all right. I felt the same way."

"There was this connection between us—do you think it's as simple as both being experiencers?" Mary asked.

"Possibly."

Chapter Twelve

Mary's heart was racing as she rounded the corner, and she saw the gates
to the finish line. She heard no one behind her but fought the urge to smile.
It was too early to celebrate both winning and setting a personal record. She
led the pack of NCAA Division II runners. She could see the official clock
counting up at the end of the finish line. 18:11, 18:12, 18:13, 18:14. She pushed
herself to run just a little faster, resisting the impulse to look back and see
how far away the second-place runner was. Even though she felt there was
no way another runner could catch up, checking would still slow her down.

Her coach jumped up and down excitedly when she had less than two-
tenths of a mile left. She allowed herself the hint of a smile moments before
she heard and felt a pop in her knee as it gave out. She fell forward, landing
on grass instead of a gravel road. She tried to get up, but her knee would not
work. Her heart broke as she looked up and saw the finish gate taunting her
less than a tenth of a mile away. She saw her coach running toward her, his
expression frightened.

She heard feet approaching her from behind. She saw another girl run past her, and the clock kept running. 18:57, 18:58, 18:59, 19:00. She started to cry. Her coach helped her up, supporting her injured side as he led her to the medic.

Two hours later she was at the ER.

"Well, Miss Deacon, it appears that you have torn your meniscus. Also, it looks like you have something just under your kneecap." The doctor pointed to a small object on the X-ray. "Not really sure what it is. Have you ever had knee surgery where a doctor would have implanted something? I couldn't find anything in your records."

"No," Mary answered and pushed on before the doctor asked any more questions. "Should I have it removed?"

"Most likely. It looks like it could've played a role in tearing your meniscus."

"Will she be able to run again?" her coach interrupted.

Mary looked at the doctor expectantly.

"Yes, but after surgery and a long recovery. My guess is," he looked at his patient, "your season is over. You need to find an orthopedic surgeon in your parents' insurance network."

Chapter Thirteen

Professor Stein was finishing her lecture. "Friday we will finish our discussion of Tolkien's experience at war and how the light tone of *The Hobbit* devolved into the darkness of *The Lord of the Rings* trilogy. Is it a utopia or a dystopia?"

Mary made a note, thinking one of the mid-term questions two Wednesdays away had been teased.

"Happy reading!"

The class got out of their seats and headed to the door. Mary took a little while longer sliding out of her seat because of the pain in her knee. Dick stepped over and started putting her books in her backpack—a ritual he had started after her injury. He was the only one who ever stepped up to help her.

"Um, Mary?" His voice quivered.

"Yes?"

"Are you ... busy Friday night? Would you like to go see a movie?"

"I would. With you?"

"Um, yeah. If that's—"

She giggled. "I'm messing with you. I would love to go to a movie with you. Which one?"

"Well, there are some dramas coming out. Um, *Get Shorty* is a comedy."

"What about *Powder*? I hear that's a pretty good sci-fi/supernatural flick. Or if you want a comedy, *Vampire in Brooklyn* is still in theaters." She watched the surprise spread on his face. "What? We met in a speculative fiction course."

November 3, 1995

Mary prepared for their date. For the first time since her injury, thoughts of her impending surgery and subsequent physical therapy were distant from her mind. Wrapped in a towel after showering, she checked the time: 6:11 p.m. She had about 50 minutes to do hair and make-up before he picked her up. She slipped on an emerald dress that ended just above her knees. It was a cold November night, so she planned on wearing black pantyhose under it. She started brushing her fiery red hair and thinking about the man on his way over to her dorm.

While she was a jock, and her sport was all other sports' punishment, she never felt like she fit in socially with other jocks. So, she did not lack attention from other jocks, but that was the problem. She didn't want a jock as anything but a friend. What her heart wanted was someone as passionate as her on multiple levels, not just the physical one. What her heart had found was a shy guy in a course on speculative fiction. In class, he had become engaging, passionate, and funny. Outside of class, the interactions were awkward. It had taken almost two-thirds of the semester of flirting with him, but he had finally asked her out.

She smiled; it was good to be distracted. The injury had left her with a mystery: While she knew *who* put the strange object there, she did not know *why*. Since that day, she had not been able to be around electronics. Something about her was causing interference. It amazed her friends and had become a joke, but she knew what it was. Out of a fit of desperation when her computer became too slow and the monitor too full of electronic snow while she was writing a term paper, she wrapped aluminum foil around her knee. If she felt absolutely insane as she did it, she felt even more so when it worked.

A knock on the door brought her back to Earth. Another knock brought her out of the bathroom. She hurried down the hall to the front door and peered through the peephole. Her date was standing there, shuffling awkwardly. She opened the door.

"Dick, you're early!"

His expression turned from anxious to confused. He looked at his watch. "Here I was thinking you were going to be upset I was late."

"Late?" Hers went from surprise to confusion. Her galley kitchen was next to the door, and she peeked at the microwave. In green numbers, it displayed 7:09 p.m. "It-it's okay. Please come in," she said, stuttering as she tried to wrap her mind around the missing time. *It can't be. Not again.* Mary tried to contain her panic.

"Mary, is something wrong? Your knee is bleeding!" Dick's voice was full of concern.

She looked down and noticed bright red blood beneath and to the right of her kneecap.

"That-that is a—" Her mind searched for a plausible answer. "Razor nick! I shaved my legs, so, um, I'll be right back. Make yourself, uh, at home!"

She turned on her heel and hurried to her bathroom. She grabbed a handful of toilet paper and dabbed the bubble of blood that covered the wound. She examined it; it was a small hole, about the size of a large gauge needle, which was exactly what it had once felt like. Three lines, each the same length, radiated from the hole. One pointed straight up, separated from the other two at 120° intervals giving it a triangular appearance. Her heart raced as she dabbed it with an antiseptic gel and put on a small band-aid. While she had planned to wear the sheer black pantyhose, she instead opted for opaque tights that would hide both the injury and any blood that seeped out of the bandage.

She wanted to cry. She thought that moving away would make her safe and untouchable, but this was more disturbing than any other encounter. She had lost time, but she had not been asleep. It couldn't be a dream. Even more than that, they left *visible*, physical evidence with the wound.

She composed herself. Putting on a happy face, she returned to her date. "Ready to go?"

She was hoping he would not ask too much about her knee. She liked Dick, but how could she be sure he would be as open and understanding as Jason and Ken?

He stood and smiled. "I am."

Offering his arm like out of another time, she took it as they left her apartment for dinner and a movie.

* * *

The little gray bastards did something right for a change! Mary thought as she was held against the wall next to her dorm room door.

Dick was holding her, his lips pressed against hers as their tongues danced. She was, to be totally honest with herself, surprised that he was a good kisser. His arms held her tight, but his hands remained respectful even though she could sense their desire to explore her body.

And she would have let them.

She was, to also be totally honest with herself, surprised the date had gone as well as it had. He was cute albeit awkward, and they walked to his car in silence. The car ride changed things. She had been worried that the thing in her knee would interfere with the radio, leaving them to either fumble with conversation or sit in uncomfortable silence. But when the radio turned on without any static, her relief was so palpable it was contagious. It seemed to set him at ease, enough that he started showing a funny side that made her laugh. She looked to the stars and silently mouthed *thank you* for the first time that night.

Dinner went so well that they stayed at the restaurant past the start of

Powder. They then took a walk around campus instead. He put his jacket on her the first time she shivered and guided the walk back to her apartment. Then he kissed her.

She thought about the hilarity that the date had gone so well all because the radio worked. Although she still wondered what it was that they had put inside her that interfered with human electronics when damaged.

Her mind was soon back to the here and now. She reached behind her and opened the door. They stumbled backward into her dark room and flopped onto her bed. His hands were all over her body, groping her through her dress. Emboldened by her soft sighs, he reached behind her and unzipped the dress before fumbling with her bra. They laid back, consumed by lust.

She could feel his desire through his pants. While she was nervous at the thought of where the night was going, she didn't find herself paralyzed with fear of being penetrated.

Neither heard the key slide into the lock or the creak of the hinges as it opened. The light suddenly blazed to life, and the sound of her roommate's voice was hard to miss.

"Mary Deacon! You *slut!*" Kayla drew out the last word in a squeal of enthusiasm at the sight of her topless roommate tangled up with some guy. "And here I thought you were a goody-two-shoes! I'm so proud," she crooned, dramatically placing a hand over her heart.

Dick turned a deep shade of red, and Mary clutched her sheets to her breasts. Then he ran out of the room. She shot Kayla an annoyed look while the other girl began to giggle and shout a loud "nice to meet you" at Dick's retreating figure.

November 8, 1995

Monday came, and Dick was not in his regular seat for their speculative fiction class. He wasn't there Wednesday either. She was getting worried, so after her course with Ken she went in search of Dick. She found him sitting on the floor in a corner of Hesburgh Library's basement.

"Dick, are you okay?"

He looked up at her, turning scarlet red before averting his eyes to the floor. "Hi, Mary. I am, uh, sorry about the other night. I'm not normally like that."

She sat down next to him. "You don't have to apologize. I had a nice time. I enjoyed myself."

He looked at her suspiciously. "Really?"

"Yes." She placed a hand on his arm, breaking the touch barrier. "Besides, I didn't want to stop." She noticed him squirming in mild discomfort. "I'm not normally like that either. I'm a virgin."

He raised his gaze off the floor to meet hers and took a deep breath. "So, is there a chance for a second date?"

"All you have to do is ask."

Chapter Fourteen

It had been a great second date; Dick had taken her to a modern update of the ancient Greek comedy *Lysistrata* by Aristophanes. In addition to the dialogue being updated to 1990s sensibilities, the costuming reflected modern fashion as well. Lysistrata was recast as Hillary Clinton.

Dick had picked the play to appear cultured. He was ill-prepared for the bawdy nature of the Athenian playwright's anti-war farce. He was relieved when Mary had found the depictions of the engorged "burdens" of the sex-starved male combatants funny.

After the play, they went for a walk.

"So why don't you live in the dorms?" she asked. "You are the only freshman I know who doesn't live on campus."

He remained silent, considering his options. "It may surprise you," he said as he stretched the truth, "but I am an incredibly awkward person. In fact, I am fairly introverted. It borders on being debilitating. So, I worked through high school and saved my money to be able to afford an apartment.

And no roommate."

"But I've seen you in class! The way you can engage our professor and other students. You're ... fearless."

He chuckled. "Yes, but only when I am sure that I know what I'm talking about. But the thing is, when the day is done, I need to recharge. By myself."

She wanted to ask some probing questions but decided against it. "So, what about spending time with me? Do you need to recharge after our dates?"

"No, actually. Being around you is very comforting and calming. You are very ... quiet."

"Quiet? What does that mean?"

"Nothing! It, uh, means you're calming."

"You already mentioned calming." Her eyes sparkled as she watched him squirm over his awkward compliment. "It's okay. We're at my dorm."

They faced each other, sharing in the moment when two people desire intimacy but are not yet comfortable with sharing their desires with one another. Finally, he leaned down and kissed her.

"Get! A! Room!" Kayla chirped as she passed the couple on her way out.

Dick blushed. "Is your roommate always so—"

"Exhausting?" She laughed and stuck out her tongue at Kayla. "Surprisingly, she's not here that often. Still, perhaps we should meet at your place more often? To avoid any roommate *interruptions*."

"That sounds wonderful." He kissed her, encouraged by her insinuation that there would be even more dates. Twenty minutes later he was happily walking home.

November 13, 1995

Dick awoke feeling out of sorts and like something was wrong. He had dreamt of his grandfather who had passed away when he was a child. Dick's ancestor seemingly attempted to issue a warning. Dick couldn't understand his grandfather; the words were garbled, unintelligible. He tossed and turned until about 8:20 a.m. when he finally decided to climb out of bed. He slipped on a pair of jogging pants and a Mötley Crüe t-shirt.

Yawning, he cracked four eggs, spilling the contents into a glass bowl. He whisked water, salt, pepper, garlic salt, and seasoning salt into the eggs. He took pride in his perfect scrambled eggs: well-done, pan-fried in olive oil, not fluffy, and moist. His stomach growled as he dumped his breakfast unceremoniously onto a plate. He took a bite, considering whether or not he would call Mary today. He was new to the dating scene and unsure of the etiquette. Was it okay to call her two days later? Should he give it another day? He took another bite, his belly still rumbling.

Knock. Knock. Knock.

He stepped to the door and peered through the peephole. Two men in suits stood there.

"Mr. Fisher, it's the police. We have a few questions."

Dick opened the door a crack, just as far as the chain would allow.

The older man displayed a badge. "I'm Detective Dante Graves and this is my partner, Detective Brodie Quint."

"Hold on." Dick closed the door and removed the chain. "Please, come in. I was just having breakfast. What is this about?"

"Are you Richard Fisher?" Detective Quint asked.

"Yes."

"Can you show us some ID?" He handed his driver's license to Detective Quint, who copied his date of birth, address back home in South Carolina, and social security number before handing it back to him.

"May I ask what questions you could have for me?"

"Did you go out with Mary Deacon Saturday night?"

"Yes." He felt his heart begin to race. "Is-is there something wrong? Did something happen?"

"Are you aware of her current whereabouts?" Detective Graves took over the questioning.

"I assume she is either in her room or somewhere else on campus."

"So, you do not know where she is right now?"

He looked the detective in the eyes. "I left her at her dorm. I have not seen her since."

"Have you called her?" Quint asked.

"No. I didn't want to appear desperate. Now please, can you tell me what in the hell is going on?"

The two detectives shared a look. "Have you been to campus since then?" Graves queried.

"Yes, I went there to study yesterday. In the library."

"Did you see Miss Deacon? At all? Even a glimpse across the quad?"

Dick shook his head no. "I'm not going to answer any of your questions until you tell me what is going on. Where's Mary? Is she in trouble?" His heart continued to race with worry over his missing friend—or was she his girlfriend now? This was as new to him as being questioned by the police.

"Mr. Fisher, are you saying you are invoking your right to remain silent?" Quint pressed.

"I am saying I want to know what is going on. Is Mary safe? Am I being accused of a crime?"

"Should we be accusing you of a crime, Mr. Fisher?" Graves asked.

He shook his head. "Not. At. All. I just want to know what, if anything, happened to my gir—I mean, uh, friend." He looked at Quint trying to resist his growing frustration.

"There was some hesitancy there. Is she your girlfriend or just a friend?" Graves asked.

"Right now, a friend. I've gone on a few dates with her. I don't know if that makes her my girlfriend."

"Did you want her to be?" Graves asked once more.

"I will not answer another question—"

"Until you have contacted an attorney?" Quint asked.

"No. Until you have answered *my* questions."

* * *

Dick had been taken to the police station and answered the same set of questions: Where is Mary? When was the last time you saw her? Did you do anything to her? Not only did the detectives ask such questions repeatedly but in all possible ways and combinations. Finally satisfied that he really did not know where she was, they let him know that no one had seen her since Saturday night and Kayla identified him as the last person seen with her.

He had finally been released and was almost home. His breath caught in his throat as he climbed the stairs to his apartment.

"Mary!" he yelled as he saw her sitting by his front door. He ran to her. "Where have you been?" He looked her over. She was wearing the same dress from Saturday. Her pantyhose were covered in runs, and her shoes were missing.

"Dick? Is...is this your apartment? What day is it?" she asked, disoriented.

"Yes, Mary, it is. And it's Monday."

"Monday? Really?" She leaned her head against the wall. "Not again."

"Mary, what happened? Let's get you inside," he said as he fished his keys from his pocket and opened the door.

Chapter Fifteen

November 13, 1995

Thirty minutes later, Mary stepped out of the bathroom wearing a pair
of his shorts, drawstring pulled tight to keep them from slipping off her
hips. The Guns N' Roses t-shirt he gave her practically fit like a dress.

"Thank you for letting me shower." Her voice was soft and oddly calm
for someone who could not remember the last 45 hours.

The first thing she had done after he helped her inside was call her parents and then Kayla. He washed her clothes and started making spaghetti.

"Would you mind making one more phone call?" Dick asked, handing
her Detective Graves's card. "They think I did something to you."

She took the card and looked at him playfully. "So, I've got something
to hold over you?" She smiled and giggled.

He looked at her, trying to decipher her intentions. "Are you joking?"

She sighed and stepped over to the phone on the wall of his galley
kitchen. "Yes." She leaned over and kissed his cheek as she began dialing
the cop's number.

* * *

After dinner, the couple sat on the couch letting *The Simpsons* play in the background. He stared at her. No one spoke. She tried to ignore his intense glare but found it too unnerving.

"What?" she finally asked, a nervous chuckle in her voice.

"I am just trying to help figure out what happened, but I just can't pick up anything."

"Pick up anything? Like a psychic?" she inquired.

He had heard the question many times throughout his life but rarely without mocking disdain. "Not exactly, I am more like a medium." He took a deep breath. "I talk to dead people." He sighed before continuing. "They tell me their stories and those of the living they are often attached to." He looked around the room. "I don't see anyone around you."

He braced himself for her to run screaming from the room as he questioned why he chose to divulge the information in the first place. Instead, she reached for him, laying a hand softly on his knee.

"Thank you for trying to help, but I don't think you can help me. You just don't have that kind of superpower." She smiled.

He studied her face as he weighed her words. "You-you're not going to run out of here? Make some sort of excuse about needing to wash your hair . . . again?"

"No." She took a deep breath. "I'm not going anywhere. Tell me about your—" She hesitated. "Powers? Gift?"

He chortled. "I don't know if it's a gift. It started when I was 10, two years after my grandfather died. He was a Marine and served in Vietnam. We were actually very close. I was even named after him. I idolized him. After Grandpa died, I started seeing this man. He looked different, but I realized it was him. He started talking about engagements with the VC and the name of his best friend. At first, it was dismissed as a figment of my imagination. I mean no one, not even Grandma, had ever met or heard of his best friend. One day the VFW was honoring Grandpa; he had built the Post's bar back.

Geoff Becker was there; he was one of Grandpa's best friends in the Post and the only one who had served with him in 'Nam.

"Grandma told Becker I had been talking about this guy named Louie Fulton. As soon as he heard that, he headed straight for me." Dick chuckled at the memory. "This guy was *huge*, especially to a 10-year-old. I told him that Louie was grandpa's best friend, at least until he got killed at Cam Lộ.

"I remember I actually made this giant of a man start trembling. He left me and headed over to my mother and grandmother. He asked them if they were sure that Grandpa had never talked to me about what he experienced in 'Nam. He never had. The man had nightmares about the place. The last thing he wanted was to burden me with the knowledge of what that hellhole was like."

A tear slid down Dick's cheek. "Turned out that Cam Lộ was not a made-up place. In the spring of 1967, they were trying to reopen a route to Khe Sanh, but it was thick with Charlie. Grandpa's unit lost 93 Marines in two months. They were operating out of a town called Cam Lộ."

Mary wiped away a tear, thinking about her own father. The war had been fought for so long; Dick's *grandfather* had fought in the early years of the conflict and her father had been drafted toward the end. "What about Louie?" she asked.

He looked her straight in the eye, tears flowing down both cheeks. "Corporal Louie Fulton graduated high school with Grandpa. They joined the Marines together. Louie died in his arms along Route 9 outside of Cam Lộ."

After giving Dick a minute, Mary spoke. "So was your grandfather the first dead person who spoke to you?"

Dick slowly shook his head. "I saw people who had lived in our homes before we did. Not many, so I thought nothing of it. I mean I was 10. But today I see them just about everywhere I go. I see them around most people." He looked at her, studying her. "What's weird is I do not see them around you. Like not at all. When you're around, it's like they fall silent. Not everyone, the ones attached to places remain. But the ones attached to people seem to hide."

"I wonder if it's because of *them*."

"Them?"

"Yes, *them*." She spat the word as she repeated it. Then she chuckled. "Are you sure *you* don't want to run? Kick me out?"

"Why would I want to do that to you?" Dick looked confused.

"You see dead people. I see—" Mary slowly took a deep breath, "I see aliens. It started when I was young. My mother has been abducted too, for longer than I've been alive." She was crying again. "They do ... things to me. My father, he-he believes I was raped when I was 16. But I wasn't. Not quite. I was taken on a spaceship. There was this alien—I think he was half-human—who used me. I was pregnant. For a little bit. Then they abducted me again, and I think they took my baby."

Taking a chance, Dick placed an arm around her shoulder.

"They come at will. They even tagged me or something before I left for Notre Dame."

"Like a shark?"

"Yes, like a shark. But I think I broke their little tag thingy when I hurt my knee during a cross-country meet. The doctor found this strange metal thing that looked like a pin with a slight bend in it. After that race, electronics would stop working if I was near them. It was frustrating."

"I don't remember anything not working on our first date."

Mary's expression brightened. "Yes! That's because—remember how surprised I was that you were early?"

Dick nodded.

"Well, I had a case of missing time. I thought it was like 6:00 p.m. or something. That cut that I had on my knee? I think that was them removing their tag."

"Is that where you think you've been the past 45 hours?"

She said nothing, just nodded.

"Do you remember *anything* about what happened?"

"No. I mean sometimes, but most of the time I remember nothing.

That's just the way it is. I only remember you kissing me in front of the dorm, then turning to walk into the building. Next, I'm on the steps to your apartment."

"Did you know where you were? Did you know they had left you at my apartment?"

"Yes. I don't know how I knew, but I did."

* * *

The sun was coming up, and the soft light filtering through the shades coaxed Dick awake. He looked down to see that Mary was sleeping, resting on his chest. He kissed the top of her head, then scooped her up and carried her to his bed. Softly he lay her down on his bed. He was shutting the door when he cast one last look back and saw her eyes were open. She suddenly sat up.

"Why don't you join me?"

For some reason, she no longer felt her previous fears about being penetrated—about sex. She actually felt incredibly ... horny.

He shut the door behind him as he stepped toward the bed. He stripped his shirt off her, smiling like he was unwrapping an early Christmas present. His hands cupped her breasts as he leaned forward, taking her nipple between his lips reverentially. His tongue teased her nipple erect. She moaned as he started kissing between her breasts, down her stomach. His fingers slipped into the waistband of the shorts, and he slowly started pulling them down, looking up to gauge her reaction.

She lifted her hips, allowing him to remove the last of her clothing. He kissed her mound, slowly making his way toward her slit. His tongue found her clit by accident, but the way she moaned and moved her hips reassured him she didn't need to know that. His tongue teased it from its hood. He felt himself growing from her scent, becoming painfully erect.

Her hands were on his head. She wanted this. Her fingers slid through his hair, tugging it. "I need you in me."

Despite his lack of experience, he managed to easily guide his member to slip gently inside her. He kissed her as she wrapped her arms around his neck. He began to thrust in and out, taken over by a lustful and bestial animus.

She felt him building inside her. She did not know how she knew, only that she knew. "I need you in me!"

The sound of her voice pushed him over the edge.

Chapter Sixteen

"Are you sure you don't want to join me?" Ken asked one last time. He paced nervously.

WVFI, the student radio channel of Notre Dame, was doing a paranormal-themed show and one of the hosts had heard of Ken's experiences and invited him on the show. He asked Mary for her opinion on whether he should accept. He even asked her to join him to share her experiences.

"I'm sorry, Ken." Her opinion was to run, not walk, away from it. Something about it struck her as a trap. "My mind's made up. No good will come of this."

"Sure, some people will laugh at me, Mary. But I know Jay! He's a friend of a friend. We've hung out before. I trust him."

"That's great, but I don't."

"Are you and Dick going to listen?"

"We're already tuned in."

* * *

"Tonight, we have a real treat," began Jay of *The Jay and Loud-Fred Show*. "We have Ken Buchwald. Student. Astronut."

Mary frowned as she heard "Loud-Fred" chuckle in the background.

"I'm glad to be here," Ken said, oblivious.

"So, you were anal probed by little green men?" Fred asked.

"Um, no. That's not all they do. And they are gray, not green."

"Anyone your father knew?" Fred followed up while Jay laughed.

"I-I don't think that's funny."

"I'm sorry," Jay said, composing himself. "It's just that you think aliens came and took you away somewhere. Did experiments. Why would they do something like that?"

"There are a lot of theories. Perhaps they are tagging humans to study like sharks or apes. Perhaps they are warning us of global catastrophe or—"

"Wait, so they are tracking *you*? Warning *you*? What makes *you* so special?" Jay asked, getting serious. "The thought is ludicrous. Why would they pick a college student?"

"I dunno. I mean who could tell? By their very definition, their thinking is going to be *alien*."

"How much do you think this has to do with your father?" Fred asked, totally deadpan.

"That's it. This interview is over."

Ken's interviewers could be heard belly-laughing as he stormed out of the studio.

* * *

Mary's eyes had teared up, listening to her friend get torn up by two second-rate shock jocks. Fifteen minutes later there was a knock on Dick's door. Mary got up to answer it and found Ken was standing there.

"Hey Mary, you-you were right." Her friend had a look that was equal parts pain and betrayal. "I should have listened to you."

"It's okay. You did nothing wrong. You just trusted someone, but we're here for you." Mary enveloped Ken in a hug.

Dick stepped over to Ken and extended a hand. There had been some tension between the men given the history between Ken and Mary. Over the past month, however, Dick had come to accept that there *had* been a spark, but a friendship was all that remained.

"I'm so sorry. No one deserves what they did to you," Dick offered.

"How do I return to class? I embarrassed myself, my family, and most of all my father."

"You go to school with your head held high, and with the support of your *true* friends like me and Dick."

"Hear, hear," Dick said, reappearing from the small kitchen with a trio of beers. "What you did was very brave. I know I could never—will never—go public with my abilities like you did."

"Abilities?" Ken asked, raising an eyebrow in curiosity.

"Dick speaks to the dead!" Mary said enthusiastically, wrapping her arms proudly and protectively around his waist.

Dick slid an arm around his girlfriend's shoulders, nodding in the affirmative.

Chapter Seventeen

Dick's palms were sweating as he pulled into the Deacons' driveway. They had become serious after losing their virginities to each other, so much so that he had agreed to drive her to Missouri to meet her parents. He was going to spend four days there before heading to his folks where he would spend the remainder of his break. On his way back, he'd swing through Laquey to pick her up.

Mary had no doubts about Dick being the one. Ever since the night they first slept together—ever since she wasn't afraid. Her fear had been gone since she came to outside his apartment. She knew. They had left her there on purpose. They had approved of him as her mate. He just needed to get through meeting her parents first. Especially her father.

"Don't worry! He's going to love you!" Mary tried to calm his nerves.

"Sure he is. He's going to know, you know."

She blushed. "He's not the psychic one." She winked and opened up the door, letting in the freezing winter air.

"Daddy!" she squealed as Travis Deacon stepped out of the garage.

He ran and swept his daughter in his arms, giving her a massive bear hug.

Dick got out of the car and stood by the driver's side, prepared to jump inside the moment her father so much as cast a threatening glance in his direction.

"Daddy, I want you to meet Richard Fisher, my boyfriend," she said, hanging on her father's arm as she led him to the new man in her life.

"Not much to look at. Pure city boy," the rancher said, studying him from head to toe and back again.

"Richard Fisher, sir," he said, summoning all of his courage to face the large, scary man whose daughter he had had carnal relations with.

Travis clutched his hand in a grip made of iron and looked down into the younger man's eyes. He made a show of studying him. "You mind if I call you Dick?" he poked in a mischievous tone.

"Of course not, all my friends do," he quipped back, venturing a sly smirk.

Travis leaned over, his lips millimeters from Dick's right ear. "Tell me son, have you had sex with my daughter?"

Dick went pale. His lips began to move but no sound came out. On one hand, he wanted to lie so this man would not kill him for sleeping with Mary. On the other hand, he did not want to lie so this man would not kill him for lying about sleeping with Mary.

"I-I—"

Travis laughed. "I'm messing with you. I don't want to know." He turned and walked away toward the house. "C'mon you two, it's too cold to be out here shootin' the shit!"

"He likes you," Mary said, taking Dick's arm.

"How do you know?"

"He's joking with you! That's something he did not do with my first boyfriend, Jason, for about a month."

"Really?"

She just nodded *yes*.

December 18, 1995

It was after one in the morning as Dick drove back to Mary's house. They had spent the evening hanging out with her friends from high school. Some had moved away to go to college. Others had stayed and gone to the local junior college. Two were in the military, serving in posts far from home. He watched her dozing in the passenger seat of his silver 1992 Ford Escort. He truly felt like he was falling in love with this part of the United States. It was silent. The dead were not as numerous here. He felt like he could relax as he cruised the backwoods roads that Mary grew up on.

He glanced up at the full moon, noticing the navigational lights of an aircraft traveling across in front of it. He slowed. Mary stirred next to him but did not wake up. He saw an open field ahead of him where the road widened, so he pulled over to look at the lights. They seemed to freeze in midair, then grow larger. Dick found himself transfixed.

The car engine sputtered and fell silent. *That's funny. I should try and restart the car, but it's okay*. He reassured himself. The light grew larger and larger until it started making a visible descent, stopping about six feet from the field. Dick got out of the car and started walking over to the fence surrounding the field.

The whoosh of cold air, having no effect on Dick, woke Mary. She looked outside and saw what was happening. Her boyfriend was bathed in red light. She threw the door open and ran to him, feeling herself becoming warmed by the light. Part of her wanted to stay, but past experience pushed her body into action. She began dragging Dick away and out from under the light.

He shook his head as they stepped out from the glow. He heard his grandfather's panicked voice in his head.

"*Dick! Dick, my boy! Get the fuck out of here!*"

"Sure thing, Grandpa!" he responded to the voice only he could hear.

Mary stood so close to the car and the illusion of safety that she almost missed the flicker of a lithe shadow in the car's headlights. She stopped short as a small, slender figure cut through the dark of night. She looked around. She whimpered.

"Too late."

Dick looked around him, and then he too saw the figure emerging from the shadows. He also saw another two emerging from the roadside ditch behind them. They were caught in a triangular pattern. He felt like prey.

"Mary, I'm so sorry," he said, gripping her hand tight in his.

"It's okay. They do what they want. I've grown used to it. I'm sorry I dragged you into my nightmare."

He looked at Mary's blank face, at her resignation and hopelessness. Something deep inside him started to boil, something primordially *territorial*. His mate was imperiled, and he needed to do something about it. Summoning his courage—born from a lifetime of communicating with the dead—he stepped up to the demure, slender creature standing before him, clenched his fist, and punched the alien between the eyes, directly on the slits that made up its nose.

The gray lifeform stumbled backward, a surprising degree of emotion and surprise on its face. Its body halted inches from the ground, then it regained its footing as if propelled upright by an invisible force field. Dick shook off the shock of what he had just witnessed and took a step toward the extraterrestrial to deliver another blow. But before he could, every cell in his body exploded with the sensation of 1,000 volts of electricity, and he screamed in agony.

* * *

They woke up with morning's first light. The chill of winter was starting to penetrate the cab of the vehicle. Their clothing was disheveled. Mary reached down and felt moistness between her legs.

"I think they approve of you," she said, trying to put a funny spin on what happened.

Dick gave her a weird look but didn't think much of it. "I just wish I could remember it." He took a deep breath. "Your father is going to be pissed, isn't he?"

Mary nodded and looked out the window as Dick started the car.

"But he is going to be very pleased when he hears you punched one."

"I thought you said he didn't believe in them?"

She giggled. "Well, we'll let my mom convince him he should be impressed."

Upon their arrival, by some miracle, her mother was the only one awake.

Carol was cooking breakfast: pan-fried cubed potatoes, scrambled eggs, cheese, and bacon. She smiled, knowingly, as her daughter and Dick entered the house. She handed the boyfriend a bowl.

"Mind giving me and my daughter some time alone?"

"Yes, uh, I mean no. No, ma'am." He took the offered breakfast and disappeared into the guest bedroom.

"So, are you going to tell me what happened last night?" Carol asked as the door to the guest bedroom closed.

"It was them," Mary replied, looking her mother square in the eye.

"Not an excuse?"

"No! I was asleep as we were coming home, and Dick saw something. He said it was a light. I woke up when he had stopped the car and got out. I saw him—"

"Standing in a red light?"

At first, Mary looked surprised, then realized who she was talking to. "I guess that happened to you too?"

Carol nodded. "I never told your dad, but he had been drinking so he claims he doesn't remember." She shook her head. "I guess they approved of him."

Mary blushed. "I said the same thing."

"Anything else of note happen?"

"Well, Dick *did* walk up to one and punched him."

"*Really*? What the hell happened?"

"They hit him with some sort of energy gun."

Carol shook her head. "Damnable creatures."

Chapter Eighteen

Dick took a deep breath as he picked up the phone hanging off the wall in the Deacons' kitchen. He listened to the dial tone until it went dead. He pressed the plunger and took a deep breath. He was about to release it and try dialing his parents once more when he felt hands on his back, one moving up to his shoulder and the other sliding around his waist. He jumped at the sensation.

"Whoa, tiger! It's just me." It was Mary's voice, extra soft from sleep.

He smiled. "Thank God. I don't think I could take being probed. Especially when I'm trying to call—" he paused, hesitating to call his parents' house home, "my mom and dad."

"You don't really talk about them."

"There's a good reason for that. My parents are insane."

"I'm sure they are not that bad."

"Mom is the reason people at Douglass Mill thought I was nuts for seeing and talking to dead people."

143

"Really?"

He took a deep breath and dialed the number, sliding the volume bar over to max so she could hear.

"Hello?" The twangy voice on the other side of the line was that of a woman.

"Hi, Mom."

"Dick? That you?"

"Yes."

"Oh." Her voice carried disappointment. "I was hopin' you was George Junior."

"I know, Mom."

"How's the internship goin'?"

"It's going great! Thank you again for setting it up for me!" He mustered fake enthusiasm.

"Internship?" Mary whispered, unaware of her boyfriend having an internship. He shook his head.

"Well, don't thank me, thank my boyfriend. How's Bill doin' anyway?"

"The President is just fine. He sends his love." He looked down at the floor, once more afraid a revelation about him would cause the woman he was falling in love with to abandon him.

"Well, don't tell your father I'm sleepin' with Bill Clinton."

"I won't, Mom. Hey, listen, the reason I called is ... Mary's folks—"

"Mary? That 'nother intern?"

"Yes, Mom, she's another intern. Listen, I'm spending Christmas with her folks—"

"Oh, so some slut is mo' important than yer family?"

"No, it's just they live up here in Washington D.C., and the president wants to keep us close. Something to do with national security."

"Aliens?"

"Yeah, Mom, and aliens. I've got to deal with some alien stuff." He shrugged, realizing that even the craziest of squirrels finds a nut from time to time.

"Okay." The line went dead.

"She just hung up?" Mary asked, her eyes wide with shock for multiple reasons.

"Yep."

"What the hell is up with all ... that?" she stammered, trying to put all the crazy pieces together.

"My mother thinks she is having an affair with the president. She also thinks he gave her $3,000,000 and me an internship to keep her quiet."

"And people around here think I'm nuts for being abducted by aliens." Mary shook her head. She stepped toward him and kissed him. "It's okay. You're safe here. Us Deacons aren't very judgmental." She pinched his butt. "At least you didn't have to lie about *everything*. The alien thing really happened."

His hands snaked to cup her ass, and he was about to lean in for a kiss when her father's booming voice interrupted him.

"Knock that shit off and get your dick-beaters off my daughter's ass!" the former Marine barked as he came out of his bedroom.

Dick instinctively jumped away from his girlfriend. "No, uh, I mean yes, sir."

Travis laughed.

* * *

Travis had to admit it surprised him that he was beginning to like the kid. After breakfast, he suggested that Dick join him as he worked the fields. He assumed he was just a soft city boy, but Travis reassessed his assumption as he watched the guy work. Dick did not flinch from physical labor, and from time to time a slight country twang slipped from his lips.

"So, what're your intentions with Mary?" Travis asked, standing in the bed of his 1500, pumping a sprayer to medicate the 20-odd head of cattle meandering their way.

Dick did not stop pumping his sprayer. "Honorable."

The first cow bumped against his side of the truck, and he sprayed a mix of water and medicine along the creature's spine.

"How honorable? The end of the school year? College? Marriage?" Travis sprayed an animal on his side of the truck. There was a long pause. "Well?"

"Honestly, I think she's the one. So, marriage I guess."

"I guess?"

Dick stopped and looked at the elder man. "We've only been dating for a month. We're freshmen in college. What if she changes her mind about me?"

Travis thought about pointing out that he could just as easily change his mind about Mary but thought better of it. He was beginning to like the kid and saw that he had a good head on his shoulders. Not rushing into marriage was a good thing; finding out that you changed your mind *before* saying I do was a good thing. It did not matter whose mind changed.

"I'm glad to hear you talkin' like that."

Dick smiled and was about to reply when movement on the wood line about 100 yards away caught his eye. He saw a gray wolf sitting on its haunches, staring at them intently. He turned to tap Travis on the shoulder and pointed out the animal.

"Check it out, a wolf."

"Nah, wolves haven't been 'round here in decades," Travis replied as both men turned to look at the wood line where Dick was pointing. "The last red wolf in Missouri was killed in 1950." There was nothing there.

"It was here a moment ago! It was huge."

"Possibly a gray wolf. They wander into the state every once a while from out of state. But I've never seen one here." He shrugged. "Perhaps you saw a coyote?"

"Perhaps."

Chapter Nineteen

March 17, 1996

Dick and Mary had taken their time returning from Spring Break at Laquey. They had perfect attendance for the spring semester, so skipping a day of classes would be no big deal. The big deal was that Travis had not only given him his blessing to ask for Mary's hand. The even bigger deal was that he also provided a ring.

It belonged to Travis's grandmother. His daughter deserved no less, and Dick was a good man. An honest man, if a little too odd for his taste, but hard-working and a man of integrity.

Dick led her through the woods to a spot where the soil had eroded away from the bedrock by eons of rain and the stream that coursed over the subterranean boulders. It was her space. She had shown him this place that first time he visited, had told him about how this was where she would come to just relax and enjoy nature. How she had even dreamed of losing her virginity there. That perfect evening did not happen at the rocks, but *another* perfect moment could.

"Mary?" he said to her back.

"Yes?" she asked, turning around to see him on one bent knee, hands outstretched toward her. A little box in hand. A ring she faintly remembered from when she was a little girl. Her hands went to her face as her eyes went wide.

"Oh my God! Dick!" she exclaimed, as tears slid down her cheeks. She extended her left hand toward her boyfriend, a man who was seconds away from becoming her fiancé.

"Mary Deacon, will you marry me?"

She nodded her head yes. He smiled slyly, refusing to put the humble diamond ring on her finger until she vocalized her answer. She began nodding even more emphatically.

"Yes! Yes! A thousand times *yes*!" she said, dramatically but earnestly placing her hand over her heart, as he slipped the ring on her finger.

Epilogue

Mary made a radiant June bride. Dick's family did not make the trip, so his friends and half of her family filled in the chairs on the groom's side. "Pachelbel's Canon in D" played as she appeared from a tent that served as her dressing room. They were being married by her Lutheran pastor.

After their vows and I do's, they left for the traditional Deacon pub crawl in Waynesville and St. Robert, the twin towns outside Fort Leonard Wood. While the wedding party partied, the family prepared the VFW hall where the reception would be held. From there, the couple would sneak out to travel North to the Lake of the Ozarks where they would be staying at Tan-Tar-A.

The Lake was a family tradition going back to the 1930s. Walton Deacon was born and raised in Bagnell, Missouri. The town was hit hard by the Great Depression. FDR saved the day—but not the town—when his administration selected the town along the Osage River as the site of a shiny, modern hydroelectric dam. It would provide jobs and electricity to the rural communities of central Missouri.

It would also start a thriving tourist industry and vacation spot for outdoorsmen. Then in the 1980s, the opening of an outlet mall would turn the tiny town of Osage Beach into a thriving small city as fishermen would begin bringing wives and children to the sportsman's paradise. As the town grew, so did the Deacon family, and each new union would be celebrated in the shadow of the dam built by the family patriarch on the remains of the town he helped found.

* * *

Dick was driving as Mary snoozed in the passenger seat. The voices had been whispering to him once more. He had heard his grandfather saying how proud of him he was. About eight miles north of Crocker, the voices went silent. He thought it was because of how sparsely populated the area was and always had been. Or perhaps it was because she was sleeping; sometimes when she was sleeping the voices would stop. He smiled, enjoying those moments of quiet.

They were getting rare, however. It seemed that whatever solace her presence provided him diminished over time. He looked out the windshield as one wooded Ozark hilltop gave way to an open field bathed in silver moonlight. This part of the country was beautiful, and perhaps someday they would own land here and raise a family. The field gave way to another wooded section as the two-lane highway dipped and meandered through a valley.

He leaned back in the bucket seat, ready for the trip to be over and to be in bed with his new wife. The oversized full moon disappeared for a moment, then bathed the car in its light as the headlights began to flicker and the Escort's engine sputtered and stopped. Instinctively he put the automatic transmission in neutral and coasted into the gravel driveway in front of a white garage detached from a white house.

Based on a true story...

I thought I would take a moment of your time to talk about the real stories in "Haunted Houses: Gateway to the West and the Beyond" and to identify where I'm making things up. Why? Partly because this is the first time I have used the *based on a true story* cliché, so to speak. I am not revealing the exact names of the people tuckerized (which in some cases flirts with becoming a roman à clef) in this story to protect the identities of the innocent—and the guilty.

THE OLD POWDER MAGAZINE

In World War II, soldiers assigned to sentry duty *did* report seeing a soldier dressed in a Civil War uniform. This ghostly figure would approach and challenge them. The man had a bloody hole in his forehead just above the bridge of his nose. It did so terrify one soldier that the man fled not only his post but the base as well. He went Absent Without Leave (AWOL) and had to be returned to JB by the Military Police (MPs).

During the Civil War, suspicious individuals *did* picnic outside the perimeter. There were concerns that they were casing the joint to come and raid for weapons and munitions. And while I am sure the number of guards was doubled, the names and national backgrounds are 100% products of my imagination. The reality is that no record of such a raid exists.

Could it have happened? Yes. Just because a record of an event does not exist does not disprove the myth. This merely means the probability that it did not happen is increased.

LIEUTENANT COLONEL MICKEY "LOGAN" DELANEY

This character is based upon an officer I have served with. He is one of several people I know, including myself, who have experienced things at JB. I took liberties with his stories about weird things that happened while he was staying at JB as a bachelor. Also, I have experienced having my ID card removed from a computer's card reader after hearing an overhead bin being open and shut.

THE BUILDING 78 SHADOW FIGURE

Most of this story *is* true and very little needed to be manipulated. A contractor was found after hanging himself sometime around 1912. I did try and find out who he was but could not find the records. There is a room on the third floor of the building that was lost to time until one day base officials opened up the walls and found a room. It was creepy because there were personnel files, books, and other strange artifacts. Additionally, people have seen a shadow figure that does not quickly disappear when spied out of the corner of one's eye. Rather, this apparition takes its sweet time fading away instead of going away in a blink.

THE NAZI IN BUILDING 28

Several times in Jefferson Barracks's history it has been used as a camp for prisoners of war. In World War II, both German and Japanese POWs were kept there. Reportedly, there are tunnels beneath JB that were used to move prisoners between buildings. However, they were not always kept underground. On a retaining wall behind Building 1, a Nazi prisoner carved a swastika in one of the wall's capstones.

The ones who behaved were allowed to go off base. Since St. Louis has a large German population that goes back centuries, some of these well-behaved POWs married local girls. This is what inspired my Nazi character inhabiting Building 28. But why did I choose Building 28? The story I mentioned regarding the three noncommissioned officers (NCOs) is true. Reportedly, they sent the lowest-ranking sergeant to turn off a light three times before finally deciding it was not worth it to keep sending the poor guy back upstairs.

The final piece of the puzzle is the master sergeant who suffered a heart attack after seeing the Nazi's ghost. I have been in Building 28 in the middle of the night. I have been the only person there. I have felt the hairs on the back of my neck tingling as if when I turn around there will be some horrifying specter that will stop my—

COMING MAY 2023

Broken Hearts and Other Horrors: An Anthology

Please enjoy a sample selection from Xavier Poe Kane's next book.

The Last Bride

Part I

The Three Serpents Pub

Hungary, 31 October 1608

A MIST COVERED THE ROAD BETWEEN THE VILLAGES RULED BY CAS-
TLE Csejte as Janos Skorzeny brought his sister home from the castle for the
final time. He considered using the horsewhip, but the putrid stench and
malignant taste of the fog caused his broken nag to pull harder and seek
a haven for the night. The lamps lit to pierce darkness could do nothing
against the obscuring vapor. Deprived of his sight, the thumps of Magdolna's lifeless body in the simple pine coffin conjured images of her withered
corpse, white from being drained of all blood.

"Blood-drinking bitch," Janos spat as he cursed the absent countess
who treated her peasants as slaves. Peasants like him and Magdolna. Despite his defiant tone, the hair on the back of his neck stood on end, his flesh
prickled, and every sense heightened after he had entered the mist.

The nag calmed as the haze lightened and the air became less foul.
Ahead an obstinate light glowed as it fought back the darkness.

"I don't remember passing anything on the way to the castle," he told
the nag, who responded by pulling her cargo toward the light. "Let's hope
they're friendly to travelers."

The fog thinned, and the welcoming glow of a wayside pub took shape out
of the darkness. As they neared, Janos could make out the tavern's sign swaying

in the still air. The words *Három Kígyó Kocsma* were carved in a neat script he could not read. Above them was a shield decorated with three coiled serpents in front of five undulating blue lines against a white backdrop. He hitched his nag, and she drank from the water trough as he sought drink of his own.

Shadows fell across dingy walls and danced with the flickering flames from the fireplace. A pot of stew boiled, belching the scent of broth, cheap cuts of beef, and whatever vegetables the tavern owner could scrounge. Each bubble popping released a bland odor that neither offended nor attracted a diner. Only hunger pangs would draw a weary traveler to its nourishment. As he moved away from the fire, Janos's nostrils were treated to the fragrance of lavender, thyme, and hyssop as each step ground the herbs and rushes strewn across the floor to hide the pub's natural damp and musty stench.

Janos's weary eyes scanned the room as he stepped toward the bar. A circumspect barkeep considered him for a moment then diverted his attention to pouring himself a drink. In a corner, their faces concealed by shadow, four men played a game. A comely wench cleaned up, gathering mugs, bowls, and utensils long abandoned by other patrons. He rummaged for a denar and slapped the coin on the bar.

"Staying the night?" The barkeep, a plump old man with long hair crowning a shiny bald head and silver beard to match, considered the coin before pocketing it and fetching his guest an ale.

"If you've got room."

"Aye, upstairs. Just you?"

"Just me." His tone betrayed lonely despair.

"This," the old man held up the silvery coin in ancient, cracked fingers, "will get ya the room and another ale. If you got another, you could have a ladle of soup and Kathalÿn for the night. She's a pain in the ass and not much to look at now, but she's a true artist when it comes to fucking."

Janos took a moment to appraise the barmaid. At the back of his mind a memory scratched for attention. It was obvious that once she had been the village beauty, but the bitterness she nurtured had twisted her into a crone before her time. "No, I think I'd rather keep my money."

"Most smart men do." The old man made the denar disappear.

"So then, what about the not-so-smart men?" Janos stared into the old man's dark, soulless eyes and tried not to shiver.

"Well, they say she could teach evil to Satan."

Janos spit at the mention of the dark one's name. The old man did not. "Is that true?"

"Let's just say . . . she's taught me a thing or two." The old man held Janos's stare for a long moment before bursting into a belly laugh. "Your room is the last door on the left." His eyes glanced at the four men gambling in the corner with dice. "Fair warning, Janos. Stay away from the table in the corner, and don't be disturbing my other guest staying upstairs. The one in the room on the right."

He sipped the ale. "Something don't add up. I've never been here before. How do you know my name? And host only one boarder?"

The old man grunted and turned his back to Janos.

Shaking his head at the man's disrespect, Janos took a swig from the mug. His gaze settled on the four figures sitting at the table in a darkened corner. He pushed from the bar top and crossed the room.

"Hold, Janos. Didn't old Ordög warn you about us?"

Janos halted when the man closest to him spoke.

"How the fuck does everyone know my name?"

The man to his right delivered the answer in a voice that gurgled as if the man were drowning. "We know you well enough, Janos Skorzeny." The man looked up from the tabletop littered with coins, five dice, and spilled ale. His eyes were all white with only fine, scantily perceptible circles marking where pupil and retina once focused the man's sight. His face was pale white while the hand clutching his ale mug was an all too natural purple-red.

"It-it can't be," Janos stammered. "You . . . you're Benedek. I-I saw you die when the hajduk burned our village!"

In response, Janos's fellow peasant removed his scarf revealing a gaping slit running from ear to ear in a macabre smile. Despite three years having passed since a guerilla's knife slit his friend's throat, the mortal wound still oozed blood, and maggots red from feasting on it undulated en masse. Janos recoiled from the sight, and Benedek wrapped his filthy scarf around his neck to conceal his mortal wound once more.

"It's been a long time, brother." The man closest to him spoke once more.

"György?" Janos asked, disbelieving his ears at the sound of his deceased brother's voice.

"Yes." His brother glared at him with the same white, lifeless eyes. The front of his peasant's cap stained black at his forehead. "Forgive me if I don't take off my cap, brother. It seems stuck on—and I don't think you'd like what you'd see if I could take it off."

Janos stared at his brother who took a bullet during the Bocskai Uprising three years before. The impossible figure—he began to wonder if they were all impossible figures—laughed while Janos searched for his voice.

"Brother! You're white as the thighs of our most noble countess." György spat a blob of spittle and blood on the floor at the mention of countess Bàthory and washed the vile thoughts down with a slug from his ale. "Have a seat. You look like you've seen a ghost!"

Janos pulled up a chair and took a seat. "Haven't I? You and Benedek died the same night!" He pointed and wagged his finger between the two.

He glanced at the other figures, their faces obscured by shadow as they averted their gaze back to the table. He could make out one, a hooded figure seated next to Benedek, was a woman. Her cloak was that of a noble rather than peasant stock. The other an old man, one whose hands had grown tough as leather through working the soil.

"You were supposed to protect your sister!" the gravelly voice boomed. "Not lead her to the dragon's den yourself." His father revealed his face, free of wound but not of blame. Eyes white, but still capable of piercing a son's soul with accusation.

Janos recoiled as if from a blow. "Father! I didn't know the Countess would be the consort of the devil!"

Old Ordög glanced in their direction as he idly wiped down a glass.

"You could've found her a nice man. Lukacz perhaps?" His father's white eyes were more piercing in death than life. Free now to see the things sons hide from their fathers. Free to judge. "No, you thought it better to ship her off to serve the dragon's whore!" The words hit harder than his father's hand ever did.

"What say you, noble bitch?" he spat the slur as he retreated from his father's venom.

Pale, feminine hands that never saw a day of labor emerged from below the table. They moved with a cold lethargy to the bow holding the cloak shut. With a gentle tug, the bow slipped apart and, as if removed by an unseen lover's hand, the cloak slid from her shoulders revealing her naked form as she stood.

Janos fell backward from his seat, crashing to the ground. An expression of horror spread across his face. He froze, unable to avert his eyes as she advanced upon him. In life, she had been beautiful. But in death, her smile was a putrid slash from ear to ear from where her blood had drained. Her lips sewn shut so her gurgling screams would not disturb her mistress's bathing. Oblivious to the pain, she opened her mouth. Coarse linen, stained brown from dried blood, stretched but would not yield before ripping through the skin.

"You can save me," her voice gurgled. Her skin grew loose as if her body were separating from itself. "In two years, the she-dragon will open her Gynaeceum. I am Zsuzska, and my mother is Anna Zelesthey. Tell my mother my only lessons will be of suffering and torment."

"You speak as if you're not dead. What kind of demon are you?"

"One who still walks among the living. Find your courage or else the only poise I shall learn from the Gynaeceum is this." As she spoke, her hair fell from her scalp in clumps. Skin sloughed off from muscles which soon followed. Organs now stripped of the noble girl's outward elegance plopped onto the pile of discarded flesh. The skeleton's empty eye sockets accused him for a moment before the skull cocked to one side in a final, ghastly appraisal before it too clattered to the pub floor.

Janos scrambled to his feet and bolted for the door.

"I wouldn't go out there. It's an ill-tempered fog. Who knows what doom lurks for you out there tonight," Old Ordög said as he poured a drink and slid it across the bar.

"And you would have me stay with those demons? One of whom is a pile—" his voice trailed as he pointed to where Zsuzska had collapsed. Nothing remained, not even a stain. He turned back to the table, and there in the shadows the woman sat, once more cloaked. "I will sleep with my horse."

The howl of a wolf, answered by the rest of the pack, greeted him as he cracked the door. He glanced at the barkeep who nodded toward the waiting drink. "It will help you sleep. Wherever you lay your head."

Janos tossed the drink back and thought better of the stable. He hastened across the floor of the tavern. As he reached the stairs, the woman spoke.

"Hurry, you only have two years to save me. Find my mother! Anna Zelesthey!"

Janos took the steps three at a time.

Acknowledgments

First and foremost: my darling Morticia. Without the support of my bride and partner in crime, this book would not have been possible.

Crafting a book is a creative endeavor and involves more than the author's voice. The voice of my editor, Kayla, lurks in the shadows of my prose. The beautiful art of Richard's interpretation of Dick and Mary gives the reader their first insight into what lay between the covers. And Haley's craft with design and layout gives the book a polished, professional look. These three individuals possess amazing creative skills that are indispensable to the success of this project.

Thanks also goes to those I served with at Jefferson Barracks. Serving with Dare-Bear, Professor, Six, Ace, Gator, Simo, and Chief (and many others!) was one of the greatest honors of my life.

Finally, there are people who I have never met that have proven invaluable to writing this book. David Goodwin's *Ghosts of Jefferson Barracks: History & Hauntings of Old St. Louis* was an invaluable resource on the history and mythology of JB. As are Dave Glover and the rest of the *Dave Glover Show* crew; Paranormal Tuesdays are one of the highlights of my week, and I'm so glad that they finally got to investigate JB!

In terms of alien abduction, the works of Whitley Strieber and Budd Hopkins figure prominently. In the 1990s I devoured their books. This is an interest that has lasted into adulthood. The past year with the revelations about the Advanced Aerospace Threat Identification Program (ATTIP) has been truly amazing.

CPSIA information can be obtained
at www.ICGtesting.com
Printed in the USA
LVHW082009050622
720528LV00009B/555

9 781087 945149